giving Up the V

More sensational reads
from Simon Pulse

Swoon
Nina Malkin

Pure
Terra Elan McVoy

Jenny Green's Killer Junior Year
Amy Belasen & Jacob Osborn

Something, Maybe
Elizabeth Scott

Lost It
Kristen Tracy

giving up the V

Serena Robar

Simon Pulse

NEW YORK LONDON TORONTO SYDNEY

SIMON PULSE

An imprint of Simon & Schuster Children's Publishing Division

1230 Avenue of the Americas, New York, NY 10020

Copyright © 2009 by Serena Robar

All rights reserved, including the right of reproduction in whole or in part in any form.

SIMON PULSE and colophon are registered trademarks of Simon & Schuster, Inc.

Designed by Mike Rosamilia

The text of this book was set in Adobe Caslon Pro.

Manufactured in the United States of America

First Simon Pulse paperback edition June 2009

2 4 6 8 10 9 7 5 3 1

Library of Congress Control Number 2008036304

ISBN: 978-1-4169-7558-8

This book is dedicated to Jessie Cave,
who dished on all things to inspire this book

Acknowledgments

A shout-out to my agent, Holly Root, who rocks the house. A special thank-you to my editor, Michael del Rosario, for being the kind of guy who is unafraid of getting in touch with his sixteen-year-old inner teenage girl when editing. Mike, you're "the Man."

And as always, to my family, for putting up with me in deadline mode, and the Tiaras (Christina, Erin, Kelli, and Shannon), for supporting me each step of the way.

chapter

1

Where does the underwear go?

I, Spencer Davis, was naked from the waist down. I'd folded my jeans and put them on the single chair in the corner of the exam room but wasn't sure what to do with my underwear.

Should I hide them under my jeans or fold them neatly on top? If I hide them, then maybe the doctor will think I'm embarrassed about my body, but if I lay them out, then he will assume I have no problem with people staring at my underwear.

There was a knock at the door. I muttered a profanity and crammed the white cotton undies under my jeans. I made a running jump toward the exam table and miscalculated the distance.

Son of a bitch!

My knee slammed into the side and shifted the entire thing a good foot.

Doubling over in pain, I pulled my knee tightly to my chest, exhaling loudly in an effort not to cry out. The nurse knocked again.

"Everything all right in there?"

"Fine," I choked out. I pressed my forehead into my thigh and took several deep breaths to steady myself. "Everything is fine, give me just a minute."

Ow, ow, ow.

I limped toward the counter, grabbed a paper towel, and held it under the faucet of the sink. Turning on the water, I shivered as it saturated the paper and ran through my fingers. Goose bumps prickled up and down my naked legs.

This is so not my morning.

I balanced on one foot and pressed the cool compress to my swelling knee.

How did I end up here? This is totally insane.

Naked from the waist down, holding a flamingo pose as my knee throbbed, was not how I wanted the doctor to find me. I eyed the sterile-looking exam table critically. Of course, lying flat on my back, legs spread open for all to see, wasn't exactly the way I wanted the doctor to see me either.

Had anyone else ever spent their sixteenth birthday in this position before (no pun intended)? I snorted. Most sixteen-year-olds celebrated this milestone birthday with a big bash and amazing presents, like a new car.

My present was my first ob-gyn exam, courtesy of my forward-thinking mother, who thought birth control pills were a girl's rite of passage into adulthood. Mom used to teach Marital and Sexual Lifestyles (aka "Dirty 230") at Washington State University. I think her technical title was professor of women's studies, but since Dad moved us to the other side of the mountains for his job, her only outlet was volunteering at Planned Parenthood and trying to educate the unwashed masses about effective birth control and preventing the spread of STDs. Because my sister was in college (she'd wisely chosen an out-of-state school) and I was still at home, I got the brunt of her educating impulses.

Like my sister before me, soon I would lie on the exam table, feet in stirrups, dying of embarrassment as our family doctor looked up my *yoo hoo*.

That thought almost made my knee injury pale in comparison. I hobbled over to the table and carefully took a seat. There was a paper drape within reach, so I covered my lap and sighed.

Another soft knock.

"I'm ready," I called out. *Ready to die of embarrassment*, I silently added.

The door opened to reveal a twentysomething blond nurse wearing blue scrubs, her hair clipped up haphazardly.

"I was starting to wonder if you were trying to make an escape or something," she joked, eyeing the window. She removed the stethoscope hanging around her neck and took my arm. "Let me just get your vitals and then I'll call the doctor in."

I liked the way she smiled and noticed that her eye makeup sparkled with glitter.

The nurse pointed to the scale, and I shook my head vigorously. "I think not."

The nurse smiled in sympathy. "Sorry, everybody's got to pay the piper."

I slowly dragged myself off the table. "You know, you could have done this when I was still clothed."

I held the drape securely around my waist as I stepped onto the scale.

"I agree. Maybe you should have let me weigh you when we started, huh?"

Totally busted.

I'd dodged the receptionist with an excuse that I needed

to use the bathroom and then snuck into the exam room that had my chart on the door in hopes of avoiding the inevitable weigh-in.

Crap.

The scale was just like the one in gym class, so the nurse pushed the fifty-pound weight marker onto one hundred pounds and looked at me questioningly. Sighing dramatically, I pushed the weight to one hundred fifty pounds. The nurse fiddled with the single-pound marker until it balanced at one hundred sixty-two. She filled in my height at five-eight, and I eyed her athletic form enviously.

It's not like I didn't know my weight. I was reminded of it every time I stepped into my size thirteen jeans. But was it really necessary to share it with complete strangers? Especially skinny ones? I wasn't sure which part bothered me more, revealing my weight or my vagina.

When the doctor knocked on the door after I was seated again, I felt my face redden and knew the answer to that question. I was so not ready for this.

I'd known Dr. Taylor forever. His office was where I'd gotten my first shots, first sports exam, and I'd visited him for countless sore throats and coughs. Now we were entering new territory in our relationship, and I didn't like it one bit.

"So what can we do for you today, Spencer?" He beamed a sunshiny smile in my direction.

I returned his smile weakly as the nurse gave him my chart. He squinted slightly as he read the entries, and I cringed as his eyebrows shot up.

"Well, well. Seems like only yesterday you were getting your first vaccinations, and now you're practically a woman." He smiled kindly at me, but I just shrugged.

What was there to say in this situation, really?

He asked me routine questions about my health. Did I smoke? No. Drink? No. Was I sexually active? No! When the interrogation was over, he pulled two metal arms out from the end of the exam table. They were covered with mismatched oven mitts.

"Lie back on the table, scoot your bottom all the way down here, and put your feet in the stirrups. There's a good girl."

You have got to be kidding me.

The drape was still over my lap but shifted toward my waist as I slid down. I had an excellent view of the doctor's head and shoulders when he popped on a mask and perused a tray the nurse had prepared next to him.

"Spencer, you're going to feel my hand on your knee now, so just relax. I'm going to slide it down and then you'll feel some pressure when I insert the speculum. Nurse, can you hand me that?"

Serena Robar

What was up with the kitty poster on the ceiling? Hang in there? Was that a joke? I wondered if anyone had died of mortification on the exam table before. The instrument was cold and intrusive. I couldn't help wincing.

"Spencer, I know this is uncomfortable, but I need you to relax. Push your lower back down toward the table. That will loosen up the proper muscles."

I forced myself to do as he asked and felt the metal speculum slide in. It was official. Our family doctor had just made it to third base with me.

"I'm going to open it up now. Very gently." The pressure increased, and I heard a squeaky sound, like a wheel that needed to be oiled.

"We're gonna need some WD-40 down here," my doctor joked.

I bit my lip in horror. It was sticking? I *had* to die. Right now.

Omigod, it's sticking, get it out!

"Nurse, pass me the mirror. Spencer might want to see what we're doing."

"No!" I practically screamed. He raised his head, from between my legs, no less. I made a point of calming my voice down. "No, I'm good. Let's keep the mystery alive, okay?"

He nodded and went back to work. He told me he was

swabbing my cervix (ew), and I breathed a sigh of relief when he finally removed the speculum, ending my torment. The nurse helped me into a seated position.

"We should have the results of the Pap in no time. If there is anything abnormal, we'll let you know."

I nodded, surprised when tears filled my eyes. I had no idea why I felt like crying. Maybe it was the relief that the "ordeal"—as it would forever be known—was over. Or maybe it was the complete lack of control I felt at this moment.

Dr. Taylor put a fatherly hand on my shoulder. "You're a young woman now, Spencer, and taking care of your body is part of being a woman."

He turned away so I could wipe my eyes in private. The nurse diverted her gaze to the chart in her hands. When I'd once again regained my composure, the doctor was writing something down on his notepad.

"I'm sending your prescription to the pharmacy, but here's a couple months' supply of the Pill to get you started."

The nurse produced a brown paper sack filled with three months' supply of birth control pills.

"Do you have any questions?" he asked kindly.

"Yes." I tried for humor. "Is it possible to die of humiliation?"

Dr. Taylor chuckled. "Well, I haven't heard of any docu-

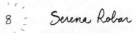

mented cases." He looked me in the eyes. "Does your boy-friend know you were coming here today?"

"I don't have a boyfriend, Doc. This is sort of a rite of passage in the Davis household. My mother thinks all girls should be on the Pill when they turn sixteen. Sort of like a pre-emptive strike. It doesn't matter that the girl in question isn't even interested in giving up the V yet. It's all part of the status quo."

He nodded in understanding. He knew my mom well enough and was familiar with her liberal thinking. "We're going to leave you alone so you can get dressed. There's some tissues if you need to clean up. When you're all dressed, just crack the door, and I'll get your mother and we'll all have a little chat. Okay?"

I nodded, and they finally left me in peace. I spent seve-ral moments immobile on the table, paper draped across my naked legs, goose bumps rippling over my body. So this was what abject horror and humiliation felt like. Nice.

Not.

I slowly slipped off the table, cringing when I felt the jelly squish between my thighs (Can you believe they lube up that metal thing?). I hobbled toward the desk for tissue, legs spread wide, trying not to make a bigger mess. The tears started again as I wiped off the offending goo. What was with all the tears?

Did everyone spontaneously burst into tears after a pelvic? That was something my sister had failed to mention.

This could very well be the most memorable sixteenth birthday in history. And not the good kind of memorable.

It was *my* body, for God's sake. I should have the final say about what happened to it. I wasn't the least bit interested in having sex, and there wasn't even a guy in my entire school that piqued my interest. I was the reasonable one. I was the one everyone came to for advice. I wasn't the girl who fell on her back whenever a cute boy said hey. I tried again to stamp down the feeling of resentment toward my mother that wouldn't be totally squelched. I loved my mother, and I knew she did what she thought was best for me, but today was, well, this wasn't it.

When I was ready to face the world again, I took one last look in the mirror above the sink and tried to decide if I looked different. My ponytail was a bit mussed, but I had naturally curly hair, so when didn't it look mussed? I quickly redid it. Other than that I looked the same.

But I wasn't. I would never be the same again.

I found Mom waiting outside the exam room door. She hugged me tightly, murmuring how proud she was of me as a woman and stuff. She even got all emotional about her baby growing up. I whispered for her to pull it together.

Serena Robar

I felt more than awkward and ready to leave, but Dr. Taylor wanted to chat with us about our visit today. I hoped he meant in his private office, like reliving it in the waiting room with my mother and five total strangers was what I really wanted to do.

chapter

2

When Mom and I left
his office (thank God) to walk out to the car, she held my arm
tightly, patting my shoulder and absently wiping her nose. I
suspected she would break down if I said anything remotely
mushy, so I stoically put my lips together.

I didn't need another scene like the one when I'd first
started my period and Mom insisted we have a "coming out"
party with the family. It seemed we Americans were the only
culture lacking a ceremony celebrating a woman's transition
into childbearing years. Personally, I would have been happy
with a trip for ice cream, but Mom wanted something more

substantial. So we broke bread at the local Olive Garden. Apparently, nothing says "sacred life-giving ceremony" like all-you-can-eat soup and salad.

We entered the car silently, and I started to feel a little guilty. Mom was only trying to protect me. Just last week our neighbor Bekka announced she was five months pregnant and keeping the baby. Bekka was sixteen, and her mom Kelly was my mom's best friend. She was a total wreck over the news.

"Are you okay?" Mom asked me in a wobbly voice.

"Yeeeeaaah." I drew out my answer slowly. "I guess so. I mean, I know it's time for me to start getting yearly exams and stuff anyway."

"But?"

"But what?"

She stole a look at me. "I sensed a 'but' at the end of that sentence."

I shrugged.

"Come on, Spencer, you can tell me. I know a yearly Pap isn't a good time, and no woman wants to spend her birthday in stirrups." She tried to make a joke.

"Then why did I have to?" The words bubbled up and out before I could suppress them. "I mean, I know the drill and all about taking care of my body and being aware and sexually responsible, but I'm not interested in having sex yet, and you know that, but here we are anyway."

Apparently, I had some issues about today.

She blinked a few times. "I wanted your turning sixteen to be significant. A new era for you as an adult." She shrugged. "And besides, they had an opening."

Lame joke. "Taking my driver's test would have done the same thing, don't you think?"

She smiled a little. "Don't be ridiculous, it takes forever to get an appointment at the DMV."

"Ha, ha, Mom." Okay, she could be mildly amusing when she tried.

"Look, I'm sorry if you felt embarrassed, Spencer. I really am. But even though you say you aren't interested in having sex, that could all change in an instant." She snapped her fingers to illustrate her point.

"I doubt it."

Her sigh filled the car. "I wish you would trust me to know about these things. I was a teenager once, and I know what you're in for. When your hormones kick into high gear, you won't be thinking clearly, and I won't be there to remind you to use a condom, but I can help prevent pregnancy."

I did not want to be having *this* conversation on the way to school.

When I didn't respond right away, she prompted, "You will remember to use a condom, right?"

"I swear, I am this close to taking an abstinence vow," I threatened with mock menace, thumb and forefinger a millimeter apart.

"See, I've embarrassed you now. Imagine having this conversation when you really *are* ready to have sex. Do you think you'll feel less embarrassed coming to me then? No, you won't. In fact, you might be too embarrassed, because we never talked about it, and decide to risk it. Look what happened to Bekka Genes."

"I am *not* Bekka Genes."

"I know that, honey," Mom reassured me.

"And just because Bekka was stupid doesn't mean when I *do* decide to have sex, I'll be dumb too."

Mom looked at me, concern etched on her face. "It wasn't that Bekka was stupid, Spencer. She was naive. She wasn't prepared for what was going to happen, and now she's paying an awfully high price for it."

I nodded grudgingly. Mom had a point. Bekka wasn't really stupid. In fact, she was in the top ten percent of our class. If anything, she was more of an intellectual idiot savant. Total book smarts with no common sense.

"I just want us to have an open dialogue," Mom continued.

"I want our relationship to be better than mine was with my mother. Especially when it comes to your body and decisions that affect it."

"What was grandma's sex talk like?"

"'Don't do it until you're married or you'll go to hell,'" my mom recited in a very strict, no-nonsense way.

"Ni-ice." So there were some advantages to having a mom who was a little more progressive. But I still wasn't going to have sex.

We drove in silence for the last couple of blocks to school.

"Are we okay then?" she asked anxiously, after stopping in front of the school to let me out.

"Yeah, Mom, we're good."

She smiled at me then. One of those smiles she gives when she is really proud of something I did or said.

"You're just in time for lunch. I didn't pack you anything, so you'll have to order hot."

I made a face. Blech. Hot lunch on chili Tuesday.

"Here's five dollars, and don't forget your note to be excused from class."

I reached for the cash and note, pausing a moment when Mom grabbed my hand and squeezed. Yes, today sucked, but sometimes growing up sucked.

"I love you."

"Love you, too, Mom." I meant it.

The warning bell rang as I entered the main campus. I was intent on my mission when Morgan Cave almost flattened me.

"Sorry, Morgan," I said automatically. Morgan was the resident goth chick in the Crew, my circle of friends, and not a run-you-over-like-a-bat-out-of-hell person by nature. She had her dramatic moments, of course, but those were usually reserved for her hair color and choice of dress.

I bent down to retrieve the backpack she'd dropped in the collision. When I handed it back, I realized she was crying, her black liner making rivulets down her cheeks.

"What's wrong?"

"Did you know?" Morgan demanded.

"Know what?" I racked my brain to come up with anything that would make Morgan this upset.

"Did you know Justin hooked up with that bitch Shelby Grant when we broke up last?"

Oh, the tangled world that is Morgan Cave and Justin Whales. Morgan and Justin break up all the time. And Justin always fools around when they are off-again. Then they get back together and Morgan discovers he played around when they were last broken up, and she ends it yet again.

Rinse and repeat as necessary.

"Are you sure?" I hedged. "I don't remember hearing that."

And technically I wasn't lying. I knew Justin had sex with Shelby the *second-to-last* time they broke up, but not the very *last* time. This was news to me, too.

"I can't believe he would do this to me. Again," Morgan fumed. Unsure what to do, I put my arm around her shoulder and pulled her into an awkward hug. Morgan wasn't really a touchy-feely person, but I thought this moment called for a hug. Her spiky red hair poked my right eye, making it water.

"It'll be okay. Justin loves you. And he didn't actually cheat on you. You two were broken up."

"But *I* didn't see anyone else." Morgan sniffed as she pulled away. "I love Justin completely. If he really loved me, then he wouldn't sleep with other people, right? Even if we were on a break. He'd wait to be with me again."

I doubted Justin interpreted love the same way Morgan did. It would be nice to think he pined for her, waiting by the phone for her call, but in reality, he made the most of their breakup time. Maybe if they didn't always get back together within weeks of breaking up, he'd be a little less of a man-whore when they were apart. He might actually worry that it was truly over and show a little remorse. But probably not. It was Justin, after all.

Morgan insisted she loved him, but no couple fought as much as they did. It was like hanging out on a soap opera set.

"You've got some mascara there," I pointed out, and Morgan swiped under her eyes, making an even bigger mess.

"I think this one might require triage with a mirror."

She gave me a watery smile. "I'm gonna touch up and see you at lunch, okay?"

The minute she was gone, I blew out a breath and continued toward the office, smirking at a picture of our colorful mascot wearing a pirate outfit over the office door.

What idiot thought dressing up a beaver in a pirate costume would make the team seem more formidable on the football field? The jokes about the Fighting Beavers were bad enough, but giving the beaver an eye patch and a peg leg? It was a wonder we weren't laughed off the field.

"Good afternoon, Spencer," Mrs. Wainscott, the school secretary, greeted me as I came through the glass doors.

"Sorry I'm late. I have a note." I pushed it toward her and waited for her to give me the orange "excused" sticky.

"Okay, dear. I've got you down as excused. You're just in time for lunch." She smacked her lips in anticipation.

I took the sticky from her and joked, "Brought your lunch today, eh, Mrs. Wainscott?"

She chuckled and gave me a conspiratorial wink. "Only the brave or the very foolish eat hot lunch midweek."

I nodded sagely in agreement. Which one was I, brave or

foolish? Today's lunch was chili beans served over corn chips with grated cheese on top. Thank the Fighting Beavers for the salad bar. I dumped my stuff in my locker and hurried to join the rest of the Crew.

We sat on the far side of the cafeteria, so I passed the academic suck-ups and band members and detoured around the tech geeks and jocks rather than pass by the GWWP (Girls Who Wear Pink) table. That was Shelby's table, and no way was I going to risk having a fake polite exchange after running into Morgan.

I arrived first, but my best friend, Alyssa, joined me a minute later, bringing her own bag of goodies.

"I had the worst morning today," she moaned. "And you missed a pop quiz in history."

"No, *I* had the worse morning ever," I corrected, then stole one of her carrot sticks. "And I mean *ever*. My mom took me to the doctor." When Alyssa didn't respond, I clarified, "The O-B-G-Y-N doctor."

"Omigod, no!" Alyssa looked appropriately shocked. This was the reaction I was going for. "Is there something wrong? Do you have a disease? Are you pregnant?"

"Yes, Alyssa, that's it exactly. I got pregnant from a toilet seat and herpes from the school pool." Sarcasm dripped from my voice, and Alyssa's expression turned sheepish. "No, there's nothing wrong. And of course I don't have a disease. Hello? Still a virgin here."

"So why go?" Alyssa sipped her diet soda.

"My mom wants me on the Pill. *The Pill*. Can you believe it? Like I'm some horny teenager who can't keep my legs together."

"I seriously doubt your mother thinks that." Alyssa watched me steal more of her carrots. "So, with this whole doctor visit thing, she's kind of saying it's okay to have sex?"

I choked on a carrot. "What? Just because I have access to the Pill, I should give it up to the next guy I see?"

At that moment, Zachary Thames plopped down at our table. Our heads swiveled to stare at him. When he realized we were both looking at him, he wiped his face. "What? Do I have a booger on my nose?"

We giggled in unison. Zach was *hardly* my first choice for a night of hot and heavy sex.

I'd known Zach since elementary school, but wasn't sure this particular conversation was the kind I wanted to invite him to join. Unfortunately, Alyssa had no such doubts. "We're talking about having sex for the first time. Spencer's on the Pill."

I gaped. "I'm not on the Pill. I have the *choice* to take the Pill, and I'm passing, thank you."

Zach nodded thoughtfully, mouth full of corn chips and

beans. Finally he swallowed and said, "I'm not ready yet either. Still waitin' for the One."

Ryan Payne chose that moment to swoop down, grab Alyssa's soda, and add, "I thought your hand was the One."

"Well, it sure beats your mom," Zach countered.

Ryan rose from his chair with mock menace.

"You totally had that coming," Alyssa said with a laugh, defending Zach. Pretending to think about it a moment, Ryan nodded and sank back down, gulping his stolen drink. When it was empty, he belched loudly and dropped the empty can on the table. Alyssa gave him a dirty look.

"So, Davis—who gets to pop your cherry?" Justin, of the on-again, off-again fame, startled me by asking his question from over my shoulder. He slid into the seat next to me, eyeing Alyssa's lunch with disdain.

Sheesh, was everyone eavesdropping?

"No one," I insisted. "Jeez, can we talk about something else other than my virgin status, please?"

"No," the group sounded off in unison.

"Pick on Ryan. Surely he slept with someone new this weekend, man-whore that he is."

Ryan had mastered the whole man-whore lifestyle and was not to be confused with Justin, who was just an opportunistic man-whore.

"That's *Mr.* Man-whore to you, and it's not easy being me." Ryan thumped his chest in what he probably thought was a manly manner. "There were two great parties this weekend. I can't be held responsible for my actions when there are ladies present."

"He uses the term 'ladies' loosely," Alyssa commented, and I smirked.

"Speaking of party hookups, talk to Tina, man." Zach came up from his lunch for just a second to impart this request.

Ryan made a face. "Why?"

"'Cause she's stalking me, wanting to know if you like her, are you going to call her, yada, yada, yada," he complained.

"Dude, if I was gonna call her, I would have, don't ya think?"

"You're such a pig, Ryan. Some girls actually expect a guy to call them after they sleep with them. The least you can do is tell her you're not interested."

"Why should I do that?" Ryan seriously appeared not to understand. "I didn't promise her anything. She knew what she was doing."

Alyssa and I gave him a look.

"For the most part," he amended. "Hey, you can't be playa hatin' when you ride this ride." He gestured toward his crotch. "That's the way it is. Anyway, don't burn bridges. You never know when you're gonna see each other at the next party, get me?"

"You both sicken and amaze me," I said. "Not an easy combination, sir, so kudos to you."

Ryan saluted. Zach rolled his eyes and turned back toward me. "Look at all the fun Ryan's having. Dodging girls, lying like a dog. Are you sure you even want to get into that whole scene?"

I looked around, desperate to find something else to talk about. That's when I spotted Morgan making her way in our direction. Aha, relief.

"Oh, Justin," I said sweetly. "I think Morgan's looking for you."

He jumped up instantly. "Hey, babe, take my seat."

Everything about Morgan was red. From her spiky hair to her flushed cheeks to her bloodshot eyes.

"Did you think I wouldn't find out?" she demanded, getting up in Justin's face and apparently not caring to keep her voice down.

Justin's brow furrowed at the loaded question. How many things was he hiding that he couldn't think of what would be upsetting her?

Zach leaned close to me and whispered, "Do you know what this is about?"

I mouthed the word "Shelby," and his face lost some color.

This wasn't going to be pretty. It was a train wreck in the making, and like spectators at such an event, the Crew couldn't make ourselves look away.

"Of all the people you had to go off and fuck—you picked that skanky whore?"

Justin was clearly confused. "What did I do?"

Ryan couldn't keep his mouth shut and answered unhelpfully, "Dude, I think it's more *who* did you do."

Morgan turned her rage on him and screamed, "Shut up, Ryan."

The offending party raised his hands in surrender.

"I didn't screw Shelby." Justin looked truly perplexed.

"Liar! Over the summer you fucked her."

"*This* summer?" Realization dawned on him. "You mean when you dumped me this past summer? When you told me I was too immature to have a serious relationship?"

"Exactly! Then you go screw that whore. Real mature."

I shared a look with Alyssa. It felt like déjà vu. Ryan, Morgan, and Justin were seniors, one year ahead of us, and Morgan had constantly dumped Justin last year. It looked like this year would be no different.

"We were broken up!" Justin exclaimed in frustration.

Tears welled up in Morgan's eyes. "It's like every time I think I can trust you, I get my heart broken."

She dashed away, making a perfectly timed exit.

All heads turned to look at Justin as the entire cafeteria watched the drama.

"We were broken up!" he reiterated helplessly.

Justin sat down heavily, and the chatter in the lunchroom started up again. I glanced over to the GWWP table, where Shelby Grant, the queen bee herself, reigned over her lesser subjects. She smirked in our direction. Well, that solved the mystery of how Morgan found out about Justin's fling. What a bitch.

"Sucks to be you, man," Ryan observed, leaning backward in his chair and popping more corn chips into his mouth.

Justin put both hands on the table, stood up, and leaned toward me.

"Don't have sex, Davis. Ever. It makes chicks freakin' psycho." Then he left in the opposite direction of Morgan.

"Back to business." Ryan helped himself to Justin's forgotten lunch. "So, Davis, who's gonna pop your cherry?"

chapter 3

Just a couple of months into the school year, and Morgan and Justin were already broken up. Again.

And apparently I wasn't the only one contemplating my virgin status either, which came as quite a surprise.

The final bell rang, and I waited for Alyssa by our lockers. We were going home together to work on our history report.

After loading our backpacks with the necessary books, we trudged out to the parking lot, where Alyssa's old Honda Civic waited.

Alyssa popped the trunk.

"So I think it's time."

I frowned. "Time for what?"

"Time for me to give up the V."

"Are you crazy? Just because I got the Pill doesn't mean you have to have sex."

"I know, but this isn't about you getting the Pill." I must have looked skeptical, so Alyssa amended, "Okay, it's not *only* about you getting the Pill. I've been thinking about it for a while now, and I think I'd just like to get it out of the way. You know?"

"Get it out of the way? You make it sound like going to the dentist or getting a shot. Shouldn't your first time be with someone you love?"

"I don't think the two things are mutually exclusive. I'm going to have a one-night stand."

I walked around and opened the passenger side of the car. Alyssa's home life was far from ideal. Last year her father had introduced Alyssa and her mom to his former mistress—and, lo and behold, their two illegitimate sons.

I still wasn't sure how it all happened, but now the two boys—whom Alyssa referred to as the Replacements—spent every other weekend at their house. Her mom had not only stayed with her dad, but she watched the Replacements when he went away on business, because he'd promised the affair was over. No one ever talked about it, which was screwed up.

In fact, their entire family was screwed up. Maybe that was why she had this screwy idea that she needed to have sex.

I waited for Alyssa to join me in the front seat. "Won't you feel weird when you look back and think of your first time and you can't even remember the guy's name?"

"Gee, Spence, it's not like I'm going to pick up some random guy off the streets. Sheesh."

I felt my cheeks get hot. "Sorry. You just kind of freaked me out with this whole discussion."

I snuck a side glance in her direction as she started the car. Alyssa was petite, half-Asian, and flat as a board. She was five months older than me but looked like she was twelve.

"The way I see it," Alyssa said, "everyone says their first time is terrible. So do I really want to remember my first *love* as being terrible? It just makes sense to pick someone with a lot of experience, and then maybe it won't suck."

"That is scarily practical of you."

"And anyway, if it does suck, then I don't have to lie to the guy and say he was great. If he's not my boyfriend, I won't have to worry about hurting his feelings."

"You got me there," I admitted. "But won't you feel weird getting naked with some guy you don't know that well?"

"Who says I won't know him well? May Valley has no shortage of guys."

"You want to have sex with someone you're gonna see every day at school? Catch his eye in the hallway and be instantly transported back to the moment when the deed got done and you said 'eh' when he asked you how it was?"

Alyssa released a long, drawn-out sigh. "Maybe we should agree to disagree on this topic and move on."

"No, I'm trying to understand. I really am." I was frustrated, because what Alyssa was planning seemed so alien. She'd never mentioned feeling this way before. "I just don't get why you would lay with some guy if he doesn't mean anything to you."

"Lay with him?" Alyssa repeated incredulously. "Next you'll be calling our first time a 'deflowering' and want to hang the bloodstained sheets out the tower window. It's just sex, Spencer. People have it all the time and don't treat it like it's some sacred act."

"So you don't think of it as sacred?"

She thought about it a moment. "No, sex isn't sacred. Awkward fumbling in the dark with a lot of uncomfortable poking? That's a memory I could do without idolizing."

"But it should be special—"

"Don't talk to me about sex being special," Alyssa snapped. "My dad had an affair and now my mom watches his demon spawn on the weekends. Is that special? Look at Justin and Morgan. Was it special when he fucked Shelby? Putting sex on a pedestal will get you hurt, Spencer. Unless you find the kind of guy who has the same old-fashioned ideals you do, and good luck with that. Otherwise, it is what it is."

Alyssa must have known that she'd shock me into silence. I know sometimes I'm a dreamer. She constantly accuses me of having my head in the clouds. Maybe she knew that I would build up my first time to some impossible level and be devastated when it turned out nothing like I'd dreamed.

Or maybe Alyssa was just damaged goods, thanks to her father.

After a few moments of silence, she asked, "Did you get Zach's notes for our project?"

"Oh, shit!" I exclaimed. How could I have forgotten the notes? I never forgot things. I was always on time and came totally prepared. I was like the Boy Scout of chicks. This morning had me more rattled than I cared to admit.

"No worries, we'll swing by his house. It's not far."

We backtracked several blocks and arrived at Zachary's two-story house in record time. We parked in front of a quaint picket fence, which kept Zach's very lazy Labrador from making even a halfhearted effort to move in our direction.

We were walking up when Zach's mom threw open the door, waving a wooden spoon in the air.

"Thank goodness you two are here. Maybe you can talk

some sense into him. I swear that boy has pudding between his ears." She moved aside and held the screen door open for us. "Hurry up, now. Don't let Max in."

I shot a doubtful glance in the dog's direction. He hadn't moved an inch since we'd entered the yard and didn't seem poised to take flight anytime soon, but I went into the house quickly behind Alyssa anyway. Mrs. Thames was not the kind of mom anyone wanted to rile unnecessarily. She withheld baked goods when she didn't like you, and that was cruel and unusual punishment.

"What's the scoop, Mrs. T?" I asked once we were safely ensconced in the family room, which looked like it was straight out of a Pottery Barn catalog.

"He doesn't want to do Math Olympiads this year. Says it will interfere with his social life." Her voice rose several decibels toward the end of her statement, and the music coming from Zach's room increased in response. She started waving the spoon around again.

I understood her concern. Zach had been on the math team since junior high and was their star player. Sure, it wasn't the "it" sport at school or technically even a sport at all, but it would look great on his college applications. We were juniors now. It was time to start thinking ahead.

"We'll go talk to him."

She thanked us as we made our way upstairs. We didn't bother knocking.

Zach's room was like any other guy's room—a complete mess. Alyssa turned down the music so we could hear each other as I kicked dirty clothes out of the way, making a path to his bed.

I stopped, hands on hips, tapping my foot with annoyance. He was lying backward on the bed, throwing a Nerf ball against the headboard.

"Just what do you think you're doing?" I demanded.

"Listening to music."

"Not that, you idiot. Math Olympiads. If you drop out now, you can't use it on your college applications. You need the extracurriculars, Zach—you don't play any sports."

"Yeah, and since when do you have a social life to be interfered with, anyway?" Alyssa chimed in.

Zach sat up in his bed and pointed to Alyssa. "That's exactly the point."

"I don't get it."

"I don't play in a band. I'm not in journalism. And I hate sports. So where do I fit in? With the math geeks? Now there's something for the yearbook." He lay back down and used more force than necessary on the next toss.

"You fit in with us." I didn't understand Zach's dilemma.

Zach snorted and tossed the ball again.

"You're gonna have to help us out on this one, Zach. Is it a problem with the Crew?" Alyssa was starting to get annoyed.

Zach grabbed the ball and squeezed it, sighing in frustration.

"Have you ever felt invisible?"

I was taken aback by the question. Zach was everyone's buddy. He had friends in all the cliques and could easily migrate among groups. A social chameleon. Invisible? Nah. I shook my head at him.

"When I'm with the Crew, sometimes I feel invisible. Outshined by Ryan and Justin. They can get any girl they want," Zach complained. "And me? I'm always the buddy. Or worse yet, I'm the math geek who calculates complex equations for the nerd squad. Now that's sexy. *Every* girl wants to be with that guy. I'm sick of being the shoulder girls cry on when Ryan screws them, then discards 'em. I would never lie to a girl to get a piece of ass, but Ryan does it all the time, and then they come to me to talk about it. Wanna know why?"

I nodded, afraid to open my mouth and say the wrong thing.

"Because I'm such a good listener. I'm such a good *friend*. Now hold my purse while I go blow some jock in the bathroom because he winked in my direction."

I couldn't believe what I was hearing. "That's who you'd rather be? Someone like Ryan?"

"Yes—no—maybe." Zach growled in frustration. "I don't know. I just know that being a part of the math nerds isn't helping my reputation any."

"Being part of the Math Olympiads didn't bother you last year," Alyssa pointed out.

"Yeah, it kind of did."

"Why didn't you say something?"

"Why would I?"

Alyssa and I shared a look that said, *Boys make no sense.*

I tentatively sat down next to Zach and grabbed the Nerf ball when he threw it. He'd grown over the summer and was much taller than me. I bounced the ball a couple of times on the floor.

"So, what now? You start winking at girls in hopes they'll pull you into the bathroom and blow you in a stall?"

Alyssa swallowed a giggle.

Zach gave a self-deprecating smile. "Too ambitious?"

I tossed the ball onto his chest and made my thumb and first finger pinch about an inch apart. "Maybe a touch."

Alyssa piped in with her own suggestion. "Maybe you could quit being Ryan's breakup wingman? The next girl who cries to you about what he did to them, just send them packing. Tell them to talk to Ryan about it."

Zach turned the orange sponge ball around in his hands.

"Bold changes require bold moves," I agreed with Alyssa.

"Be less of a nice guy?"

"Yeah, be a dick once in a while. Chicks like that."

"Well, at least the kind of chicks who would sleep with guys like Ryan," I amended. "But maybe you shouldn't write off the math team just yet. You really do need it on your applications, and it will help with scholarships. And who knows? You might meet some cute math chick who gets off on smart guys at your next competition, and she'll drag you into the bathroom and have her way with you."

"A man can hope."

Alyssa plopped down on the other side of him.

"If I was a skanky whore, I would so blow you in the bathroom, Zach," she declared in earnest.

"Me too," I added.

"So, if you two *were* skanky whores, you wouldn't see me as just a friend?" Zach was amused.

"No way," I assured him. "You'd be a man-whore all the way. We'd be crying on Ryan's shoulder about the horrible way you treated us—"

"After detailing how hot the sex was," Alyssa interrupted.

"Oh yes, what she said. Ryan would look to *you* for sex tips and think of you as a god."

Zach sat up and raised his hands for us to stop.

"You had me at blowjob in the bathroom. I'll stay on the Math Olympiads."

chapter 4

After we saved Zach's post–high school career plans, we went over to Alyssa's to work on our history project. No Replacements in sight, thank God, because nothing said "awkward" like trying to make conversation with your best friend's mother when the proof of her husband's infidelity was playing cars at your feet.

"SoonYi? You and Spencer eat dinner first, study later." Alyssa's mom always called her by her Korean name, even if her father and everyone else called her Alyssa.

Mrs. Hobbs also cooked constantly, probably feeling

that food equated love. Usually it smelled like cabbage and something I couldn't distinguish, but today it smelled like barbecue.

"Mom, we're not hungry. We really need to get this project done. We'll eat later."

"No later. Now. I make good food. Spencer, you sit and eat. You big girl. Like good food. Come." Mrs. Hobbs had lived in the States for the past fourteen years, but her English never seemed to improve. I found it charming, unless she was commenting on my size. I guess it's a cultural thing.

Last Christmas she told me I was getting fat, in front of the entire Crew. She didn't mean it to be cruel, just a statement of fact. Either way, I preferred not to hang out at Alyssa's house. Seriously, it was hard enough having a best friend who wore a size one. I didn't need her mother commenting on my thighs as if she was noticing the weather.

"No, Mom, really, we're not hungry and we have to study." Alyssa hustled us out of the living room and into her room before her mother could reply.

She closed the door and leaned back against it, letting out a whoosh of air. "What is it with moms and shoving food down our throats?"

I shrugged my shoulders. Zach's mom had made us eat three cookies each before we left and even filled up a bag for later. There were worse things a parent could do than feed your friends. Like call them fat. But I digress.

We plopped down on Alyssa's lavender bedspread and pulled books out of our bags.

"Do you have them with you?" Alyssa asked, attempting to peer inside my backpack.

"Have what?" I pulled it away from her and dug through, trying to find my favorite pen.

"You know, the pills?"

I sat up quickly and almost knocked her out with my head.

"No, I left them in the car with my mom. Why?"

She shrugged indifferently. "I've just never seen any up close before."

Truth be told, I'd seen my fair share. Mom always brought home different packets from Planned Parenthood to educate us on how they worked. When to take them and why you could skip the green ones if you wanted. Dad buried his head in the paper or hid in their bedroom during Mom's spontaneous sex education lectures. You know, he did what *normal* parents do when faced with discussing sex with their teen. Got embarrassed and acted all uncomfortable.

"When you come over next, I'll show them to you."

She nodded, and we opened our books. About ten minutes

later she jumped from the bed and stood in front of the full-length mirror.

Exasperated with her uncharacteristic attention deficit, I asked, "What are you doing now?"

"I have no boobs." She placed her hands on her hips and turned sideways to emphasize her point.

"Yes, you have no boobs. Can we get back to work here?"

She ignored my plea and ran her hands up her chest, clutching her small breasts. She pushed them together, causing her tee to form a small V of material.

"I could have cleavage if I taped them together."

"Girlfriend, you wouldn't have cleavage if you *glued* them together."

She gave me a dirty look and let go of her breasts. Sighing deeply, she dropped back down on the bed, moaning, "Why are some granted so much and others so little?" She stared pointedly at my bust.

I laughed. "When you have an ass the size of mine, it seems only fair to have boobs to even things out. At least you have a great butt."

And Alyssa did. It was perfectly shaped, and boys certainly noticed it. Unfortunately, when she turned around, looking like an elementary student, it squelched most male interest.

"Maybe I should try wearing makeup? Dress more . . ."

"Skanky?"

"I was thinking provocative, but whatever gets the job done."

"Oh, no," I groaned. "This losing-your-virginity thing didn't just become a goal for you, did it?" Alyssa was unstoppable when she made a goal. Tenacious didn't even begin to describe it.

She contemplated my statement a moment and then shrugged.

"Please don't. You'll become obsessed. You'll fill that notebook of yours with strategies to achieve your evil end, and I'd hate to read your to-do list on getting laid."

She laughed and we went back to Henry VIII and why he had such a tough time keeping a wife.

Alyssa drove me home, but not before I was force-fed Korean BBQ. At home, my mom waited for me as I walked through the door.

"Hey, Mom." I dropped my backpack inside the door.

"Hi, baby, how are you feeling?" She hugged me, and her gaze searched my face for some inkling of my mood.

"I'm fine, Mom, really. I've gotta shower."

She let me go, seemingly satisfied that I had not decided to sleep with the first guy I saw after getting the Pill nod-of-approval, and went back to the kitchen.

In my room, I kicked off my sneakers and sank into my

computer chair. I stared at the brown bag of pills Mom had put on top of the dresser.

Who knew that such an innocuous-looking bag could hold such controversial contraband? I guess it wasn't technically contraband if I had permission from the powers that be to take them, but still, I felt weird having them out in the open. Would a guy leave condoms on his dresser for anyone to see? I thought about Ryan. There was a guy who probably bought in bulk.

I logged on to my computer and was instantly bombarded by IMs. Sighing, I waded through the greetings. Alyssa just wanted to say hi, since I'd just seen her. Morgan wanted to talk about Justin, and Zach was having second thoughts about Math Olympiads.

Same ol', same ol'. I was the one the rest of the Crew came to for advice and help. I wasn't sure why, exactly—after all, I'd never had a boyfriend. But I was the go-to girl when a relationship was in crisis. Go figure.

I had a bit of sympathy for Zach feeling like he was just a buddy. Maybe we were more alike than I'd noticed before.

I decided Zach would be the easiest to deal with first.

ZachAtck: I'm not sure I made the right decision about MO.
Spence: Hot math chick. BJ. Bathroom.

ZachAtck:	Ah yes, now I remember. Thanks. ☺
Spence:	NP

Alycat:	Morgan's been asking me all sorts of questions about what she should do with Justin. You might want to be invisible to her right now.
Spence:	Ha, too late.

Gothgrl:	Spencer help! I just don't know what to do about Justin. What if he starts dating Shelby? I don't think I can handle that.
Spence:	U could get back together . . .
Gothgrl:	WTF?!

I sighed heavily and logged off. I wasn't in the mood to be Dr. Phil.

I revisited the conversation I'd shared with Alyssa and her comments about it being time for us. What would my first time be like? Was I being unrealistic to assume it would be romantic and wonderful with the guy I loved? Did I really have my head in the clouds?

It was time to get a second opinion. I headed for the kitchen, where Mom was cleaning up.

"Mom? Would you say I have my head in the clouds?"

"No, not really. I mean, sure, you have your daydreaming moments, but most of the time you're quite sensible."

"Sensible?"

"Of course. Why do you think all your friends come to you for advice? You can sort things out without emotional bias."

"So I'm unemotional?"

"For heaven's sake, Spencer, I'm not saying that at all. I'm complimenting you on your levelheadedness. When I ask you to do something, it gets done. You don't give way to hysterics if you don't get what you want. You accept things the way they are. These are marvelous qualities."

I left the kitchen in a morose mood.

Sensible, responsible, accepting. Nails in my social coffin. Unemotional equaled passionless in my book, so what could I expect? I'd never had a great love or even a lukewarm one. I read romance novels, but I couldn't expect a guy to make my heart palpitate and pulse race. That was fiction. I always thought I'd end up with a guy who was easy to get along with, someone who made me laugh, who I could be myself around.

Was there something wrong with me that I wasn't obsessed about the physical side of relationships? I didn't dream of carnal lovemaking on the beach because, quite frankly, it sounded uncomfortable. I hated it when I got sand in my shoes, never mind where it'd be after a rendezvous in the surf.

And the thought of someone seeing me naked? Snort. Forget it. I went out of my way to clothe myself in layers to hide my figure, not to wear skintight shirts to accentuate it. No one was seeing my muffin top, thank you very much.

Argh!

Why did this suddenly matter so much? I stole a look at the dresser. I knew why. Because I now had a brown sack filled with the Pill, that's why.

They mocked me as I took my clothes off to shower, trying not to look in the mirror. Every time I saw myself naked, I remembered changing next to Shelby Grant last year before gym. I'd pulled my shorts up with a little jump and she'd stared at my thighs.

"You can stop jiggling now."

What. A. Bitch.

I entered the bathroom, loving that I didn't have to share it with my sister anymore, since she was at college.

I tugged out the ponytail holder and massaged my scalp. My hair was naturally curly and long. I had a flat iron and could straighten it instead of wearing it pulled back, but that took *forever*. I suppose swiping some mascara across my lashes would make my blue eyes stand out, but again, the laziness factor usually won out. At least I wore my contacts to school most of the time.

I turned on the water and waited for it to get hot. Dad installed a tankless water heater last winter, and it rocked. Endless hot water. Like heaven.

I scrubbed myself from head to toe, wondering what it would be like to date someone who thought you were beautiful with and without clothes on.

In the age of Internet porn, boys my age were pretty savvy about a girl's naked body. Not because they had more experience, they just knew how to click, "Yes, I am eighteen or over." The girls on those sites were always in great shape and beautiful. Tell me, when was the last time you saw a *Girls Gone Wild* video that featured a chubby, plain girl? That's right. Never. Maybe if they featured someone like that once in a while, we "typical" girls wouldn't hyperventilate at the mere thought of unclothing in front of our significant others.

I finished my shower and toweled off. I rolled the towel, turban-style, over my wet hair and dared a quick glance in the steamy bathroom mirror.

Wouldn't the guy who unwrapped *this* package be in for a shock? Forget *Girls Gone Wild*. More like *Girls Gone Lumpy*. I reached for pajamas and viciously shoved my feet into the legs, snapping the waistband.

I pulled on a tank top. There was no way I was letting any guy see me naked. No freakin' way. I left the bathroom and took a running jump onto the bed. I grabbed my book off the nightstand and opened it to where I'd left off.

After four attempts at reading the same page, I put it down. I couldn't concentrate on the words. I kept thinking of the moment I finally unveiled myself for the first time, and the mysterious guy would shake his head in disappointment, or worse yet, disgust.

Yeah, there was no way I was getting naked for a guy. I stuck my tongue out at the brown bag on my dresser. So there.

Serena Robar

chapter 5

The next week seemed like business as usual, except Alyssa was trying to dress seductively, and I was convinced everyone at school knew my secret. I'd see girls, heads together, whispering, and I just knew they were debating my virginal status. *Will she or won't she?*

Or maybe they were talking about how ridiculous Alyssa looked wearing skintight shirts that accentuated her lack of curves. Thursday's attempt at a low-cut button-up was far from successful, so by Friday she'd decided to forget the sexy clothes and stick to styling her hair and applying makeup. It was a sound plan.

Unfortunately for me, my virgin paranoia grew by leaps and bounds. I watched my history and science teachers chatting as they entered the teachers' lounge, I assumed the worst. When I caught their eyes and they smiled, I was positive. There had to be a betting pool among the teachers on when I'd give in and finally put out. Did they have the chart on the wall in the teachers' lounge? Did they have dates/occasions that seemed more likely than others? Homecoming? Winter Formal? The next Spirit Day?

I wonder what kind of odds I'm getting?

"No one has a betting pool. Now stop being so melodramatic," Alyssa insisted at lunch, nudging my attention away from the door of the teachers' lounge. Today she wore dark brown eyeliner that really made her eyes stand out.

"Yeah, Davis, the teachers aren't going to throw their money away on a sure thing."

Ryan slid in next to Alyssa and made a grab for her soda, but she countered with an elbow to the ribs.

"Ha, ha," I groused. Ryan thought I'd spread my legs by Winter Formal and in first period had even offered to be gentlemanly about the whole thing and do the deed himself. My reply was to swiftly slam my English lit book on his hand. His knuckles were still swollen.

Justin arrived and took the seat next to mine. He put a

protective arm around my shoulder and scolded Ryan for his insensitivity.

I smiled in gratitude until he said, "And besides, if anyone is going to service Davis here for her first time, it should be me. I've known her longer."

I shrugged off his arm and flipped him off.

"That's right, baby, I'm number one. You know you want to find out."

The boys laughed hysterically at their own joke as I did my best to ignore them. Where was Zach when I needed him? He was the one male voice of sanity in the Crew, and today he'd decided to sit with a small group of giggling sophomore girls. WTF?

Alyssa noticed my stare. "Looks like Zach's taking our advice to heart."

"He's being a dick?"

"Not sure, but he *is* putting himself out there and getting out of Ryan's shadow." She whispered the last part to avoid being overheard.

Ryan noticed our focus on the sophomore table and frowned. "What's Zach doing over there with Sydney Porter?"

"Eating lunch," I answered drily.

Sydney playfully slugged Zach in the shoulder and then stroked the spot. I frowned. When had Zach developed broad shoulders? Had he always been like that? No, I didn't think so. Maybe that workout bench in his bedroom wasn't a laundry bin, despite being draped with clothes. Maybe he actually used it.

Sydney was pretty, with dark hair and brown eyes. She was very smart and captain of the JV volleyball team. I noticed Ryan's frown. Obviously Ryan hadn't hit that yet—or maybe he'd tried and got shot down. Was he worried that Zach would succeed where he had failed?

There was another eruption of laughter, and this time Sydney pulled Zach down toward her (she was tall, but Zach was at least six feet) and gave him a big kiss on the cheek. He flushed and glanced in our direction. Alyssa gave him the thumbs-up, and I attempted a weak smile. Did Sydney really have to hang all over Zach and make such a big deal over his muscles? They weren't *that* huge. Jeez, I hadn't even noticed them until right this second.

The lunch bell rang and everyone scattered. Everyone except Justin and myself. I had study hall after lunch, so no need to rush. Justin seemed to have something to say. Probably something to do with Morgan, who hadn't come to school today.

I couldn't have been more wrong.

"Spence, you know we tease you about this whole virginity thing, but I want you to know, *I'm* there for you."

I smiled. "I know you've got my back, Justin."

He looked startled and then let out a bark of laughter.

"What's so funny?"

"When I say I'm there for you, Davis, I mean I'm *there* for you. Morgan and I are on a break, and I think it could be pretty hot, don't you think?"

Surely I was misunderstanding him. "Say again?"

"Look, we've known each other forever. You're the one we all look to when we need help or advice. Now it's time to return the favor. I'd be gentle, and I promise"—he grinned arrogantly—"it wouldn't suck."

"Are you offering to service me?" I sputtered.

He gave me one of his lopsided smiles that made girls forgive him almost anything. "Come on, Davis. You've never wondered what it would be like between us? You've never even *thought* about it?"

"*You* want to have sex with *me*?" This wasn't about taking one for the team. He acted like he was really attracted to me.

Apparently, I'm slow on the uptake. Shock does that to a person.

He laughed. "Davis, I've been dying to get you naked since the summer before eighth grade, when we all went swimming together and it was obvious you'd had a growth spurt."

He was referring to the too-small bathing suit incident,

of course. The Crew had met at Ryan's house for an end-of-summer pool party, and the only thing I had was last year's swimsuit. My body had exploded in the summer months, and I guess I was in denial. Shopping for swimsuits is emotionally taxing, and I so didn't want to do it.

When Alyssa and I arrived, the Crew was already in the water. I was the last to take off my tee and shorts, when suddenly the laughter in the pool faded away. The boys' eyes bugged out, and the girls had their mouths hanging open.

I looked down at my once demure one-piece suit and saw what they saw.

My cup runneth all over the place. I mean, I was barely contained, as it were. I'd quickly pulled my tee back on and jumped into the water to hide my embarrassment.

When I resurfaced, everyone was back to normal except for the furtive glances from the boys when they thought I wasn't looking. That day was burned forever into my mind. It was the reason I still wore layers of shapeless shirts. As Alyssa would say, I was blessed with abundance, but I viewed it as more of a curse.

We were alone in the cafeteria now. Justin leaned toward me, capturing the strings to my hoodie so I couldn't back away.

Not that I had any plans to back away. I was in too much

shock, and I hate to admit it, more than a little intrigued at the turn of events. Justin was the lead singer in his band. He was hot in that bad boy/punk/sometimes goth way. He had longish, spiky blond-brown hair. He was the male, nondyed equivalent of Morgan, and half the girls in the school waited with bated breath for Morgan to dump him so they'd have a shot. But Justin was offering himself to me. Me?!

My eyes widened as his face moved closer. Was he going to kiss me here at school? Anyone could stroll by and see us, but I still didn't move. I couldn't. Things like this didn't happen to girls like me. Boys like Justin made passes at girls like Sydney Porter, not Spencer Davis. Never Davis.

His mouth hovered just over mine, our eyes locked, and he whispered, "I just want to make your body feel good."

Then he backed away, gave me a sexy smile that made me catch my breath, and released the strings of my hoodie. I practically fell off the seat when he let go, so I must have been trying to back away. But for the life of me I didn't remember moving at all. I couldn't form a coherent thought, much less an escape plan.

"I, uh, I . . ." I stammered at Justin now, still completely sideswiped.

"Don't sweat it, Davis, I understand." That sexy smile morphed into a goofy grin.

"You do?"

He chuckled. "Yeah, I knew the answer by the look on your face. As much as the idea intrigues you"—his eyebrows wiggled suggestively—"you gotta have love. It's who you are."

Oh. My. God.

I'd never been interested in any boy above the fleeting *Wonder what he's like?* thought, but at that moment my heart raced, my hands were sweaty, and I tingled in some pretty telling places.

I'd known Justin forever, but he was out of my league. I didn't harbor any secret crush or delude myself into thinking he might be remotely interested in me, even in some parallel universe. Justin was meant to be with someone like Morgan. Someone who shone in the limelight and was comfortable there. I was nothing like that. I hid behind oversize sweatshirts and witty sarcasm. But right at this moment I felt stripped of all those defenses.

Justin had made a point of letting me know that he saw through my disguise and would be more than willing to explore what I tried so hard to keep hidden.

"I, uh, I . . ."

He pulled me into a hug, laughing.

"Breathe, Davis. It's all good."

I took his advice, pushing the air out of my lungs with force. "No hard feelings?" I ventured.

His embrace tightened. "Nah, it's time for me to get back together with Morgan anyway. Yeah, we're fucked up half the time, but somehow we make it work."

I let him go but couldn't step away as he continued to hug me, even going so far as to run his hands down my back, pulling me closer to his chest, if that was at all possible. Realization dawned too late.

"Uh, Justin? Are you copping a feel?"

He laughed again and released me. "Hell yeah. If I don't gets to play with 'em, I at least wants to feel 'em."

I smacked him upside the back of his head. "You are *such* a pig."

He grinned devilishly. "Yeah, but you were tempted. Admit it."

"Hah!" I responded, thought it lacked the indignation that should have been there.

Justin leaned forward and kissed me quickly on the lips. Very fleeting. Just a slight sensation that was gone before it even registered. My eyes widened.

"What was that for?"

"Just because I wanted to. You know you're one of a kind, don't you, Davis?"

"Thank God for that. Not sure the universe could handle another neurotic mess."

He looked completely serious for a moment as he grabbed the strings to my sweatshirt and stared into my eyes. He wasn't going to kiss me; this vibe was totally different.

"I think the world could stand a lot more Spencers in it."

And I could tell by the way he held my gaze that he meant it. In the school lighting, his eyes looked more blue than gray. Not green at all. But they were still pretty.

I gave him a genuine smile in return.

"Now walk me to math class, and tell me how I should go about getting Morgan back. It has to be something outrageous. She loves that kind of shit."

And we walked side by side down the hallway, me listening to him and offering advice when appropriate, and him suggesting one ridiculous scenario after another, like nothing had changed. But I felt different somehow. I walked a little taller and stayed at his side instead of trailing behind him as he talked. I felt more like his peer. Justin was one of the coolest guys in the school, and I no longer felt like it was a freak of nature to hang out with him. We were friends. Equals. And it felt good.

chapter 6

Alyssa met me at my locker at the end of the day. "So who do you want to ask you to Winter Formal?" Alyssa kept her voice low.

"I don't know, I'll probably go with Zach like I do every year." Zach and I had a standing date for major school dances. If no one asked us, or if we had no interest in anyone, we went together. We had a blast, and there was no pressure for a good-night kiss.

She looked over at Zach and Sydney. "Don't you think it's time to put away the security blanket that is Zach and get a real date?"

I gave her a dirty look.

"Anyway." She ignored my expression and continued, "I think he's going to ask Sydney Porter. He seems to be laying a lot of groundwork in that direction."

Which was true, unfortunately for me. I had nothing against Sydney personally, except I couldn't see them as a couple. She was sunshiny, fruity Starbursts, and Zach was chocolaty nougat. Two great tastes that didn't belong together.

"If that happens, you and I can go stag," I offered.

"Hello? Excuse me, but I plan on having a date that night."

"I thought we agreed that having sex that night wasn't going to be a goal for us."

"What does sex have to do with it?" Alyssa protested. "I just want a real date, for crying out loud. Why do you think I am getting up forty-five minutes early every morning to do my hair—which is a bitch, by the way—and makeup? I'm trolling for a man, Spencer." She fluttered her eyelashes at me until I laughed.

"Okay, I applaud your commitment and sacrifice of sleep to dazzle a potential date, but I'm not sure I'm willing to do that. Do you have any idea how long it takes to blow out my hair? I'd have to get up at three in the morning."

"Hmm, you have a point. Hey, can I still come over tonight?"

"Of course. Season two isn't going to watch itself." We were watching *How I Met Your Mother*, our latest entertainment obsession.

"By the way, do you think Justin and Morgan are ever going to get back together?"

I glanced surreptitiously in Morgan's direction. She was shooting eye daggers in Justin's direction, provoked by his agreeing with Ryan's crass observations about the opposite sex. "The tension between Morgan and Justin is still too intense."

"True," Alyssa agreed. "I actually thought they'd get back together by now. I know Justin wants to, but Morgan doesn't seem ready yet."

"The boy did sleep with Shelby Grant. Give the girl some time." We both stole a look at Shelby's table, where she was pantomiming Morgan glaring at Justin.

"Or a lobotomy," Alyssa added.

Destiny reveals itself in strange ways. My destiny was revealed by Mother Nature, in one of her rare moments of clarity in the usually wet and cloudy Pacific Northwest. I was hiding outside during lunch, avoiding the whole Justin-and-Morgan drama, finishing a sandwich. As I looked out toward the parking lot, the clouds chose just that moment to part. The sun's brilliant rays beamed down to reveal a creation of male perfection emerging from a red truck.

The heavens had literally opened up and spotlighted my destiny.

If my mouth hung open, I wouldn't be surprised. I finally understood what every romance writer meant when they described the first meeting between the hero and his heroine. His beauty literally struck me speechless. Tousled brown hair, great skin, strong jaw, and full lips. And what about that body? I could tell from here that he was built. Ryan was the only other guy I knew who was as contoured and muscular. Ryan always wore tank tops or fitted tees to show off his pecs and arms, but this boy had on a long-sleeved shirt, and I could still tell that he was well defined beneath the loose fabric.

Drool could very well have run unchecked down my chin. My heart beat fast, and my stomach rolled like a front-loading washing machine on the spin cycle. This boy was beautiful. Achingly beautiful. Suddenly I knew exactly what all the fuss was about. This was it—the reason girls followed guys around like puppy dogs and would do anything, including have sex, to keep their interest.

For the first time I felt physical desire for another person, for this newcomer to May Valley High. And I knew it was

desire, want, lust, because I'd never felt so strongly about any-one before. It made what I was experiencing for Justin seem almost childish in comparison. I wanted to touch this boy's shoulders and feel his arms around me. I just knew he'd smell like the ocean, and if I buried my face in his neck and inhaled deeply, my knees would weaken. As assuredly as I knew my own name—which I clearly couldn't tell him if he asked, because of the whole struck speechless thing—I knew this boy was the One.

He wore jeans like he was doing them a favor, and in response, they clung to him in appreciation. His rock-hard thighs strained against the denim. An athlete's body. He walked toward me with purpose, burgundy backpack slung over his shoulder.

I prayed he felt it too. That when his eyes met mine, this inexplicable force would capture him and draw us together. He would know the universe had decreed that I was the One, the girl he'd been waiting for, and we would be sublimely happy if only we could be together.

But first off the dude had to *notice me*.

Closer he marched, and closer. My mind emptied of all thoughts. Well, all thoughts but throwing myself into his arms and raining kisses all over his exposed skin, which would have made for a very awkward introduction. I strained to keep my body from leaping off the outdoor picnic table and catapulting toward him.

Finally he stopped in front of me and spoke. I couldn't understand what he said, because he had the greenest eyes I'd ever seen on another human being. Sure, Justin had gray eyes that could look green in certain light, but not like this. Not like the endless meadows of spring.

I cocked my head to the side to see if he looked just as perfect at an angle (he did, of course). He nodded his thanks and turned to leave.

Wait! Don't go, my mind screamed. *Don't you feel it too? We are meant to be together. Destiny has decreed it, for crying out loud. I must be with you always!*

He'd spoken to me. I knew it. What had he asked me? I tried to concentrate but couldn't seem to recall the words that left his perfect lips until his amazing body went through the school doors. What was it? What had he asked me?

I think it was something about the office. Yes, maybe which way to the office? That was it. And what had I done? I'd responded by cocking my head to the side. He seemed to take that as an answer. He must have misconstrued my cocked head with nodding in the direction of the front doors.

Oh. My. God.

I'd inadvertently answered his query without even being

conscious of it. Didn't that mean we were destined to be together? Wasn't that proof I was his soul mate, the one who could answer his questions on a subconscious level? We were *connected*. I pulled my hands toward my chest, verifying that the palpitations were real. This boy made my heart go pitter-patter.

Mom was right. Nothing prepares you for when it happens. You never know and can't help yourself when it strikes. It *was* like lightning. I knew it then, as certainly as I knew the sky was blue and the sun was yellow. This boy would be my first time. He was "the One."

My body shivered as an icy breeze seemed to cut through me. It was preordained. The heavens had opened up and bathed him in golden light before me. I couldn't ignore the sign. To do so would be at my own peril. I mean, it was a sign from *God*, and you don't ignore signs from the Almighty.

The bell rang, so I gathered my lunch remains and headed through the double doors. A quick glance to my right told me that he'd left the office. I tossed away my trash and met Alyssa at our lockers.

"I'm sorry I didn't go outside with you for lunch, but it's freakin' freezing today and I have on a skirt."

I noted her miniskirt and admired the color of her legs. She always seemed to have a tan, and I was always frog-belly white. Another contrast between the two of us.

"Did they get back together?" Alyssa craned her head to look for Justin and Morgan, but gave up when she couldn't see over the heads of any students. Being five foot nothing meant she had a hard time seeing any distances in the hall. She could never find anyone—and worse yet, she couldn't hide from them either. How do you avoid someone if you can't see them coming?

"Not that I know of, but I think they will soon." And who cared about Morgan and Justin when the new boy would be in the lunchroom?

"Yeah, I think so too. See ya."

chapter

7

I *didn't have to wait*
long to get another glimpse of My Destiny. We shared fifth
period together. Chemistry. How apropos was that?

He sat in the empty chair next to me (God, I love flu
season), just as perfect as I remembered. Suddenly I wished I
had worn something other than my U of Dub sweatshirt and
jeans. At least I wasn't wearing my glasses and had even been
inspired to put on mascara and lip gloss this morning, since
Alyssa was going to all the effort.

"Hi again," he said, shocking me.

"Uh, hey," I responded lamely. The silence stretched for
a moment. "So, it looks like you found the office."

OMG. I am *such* a loser.

"Yeah." He chuckled. "I'm golden." He held up his class schedule, and I noticed we had sixth period together as well. Advanced art class.

"How'd you get into art?" I sounded shocked. Advanced art required prior approval from the art teacher and a portfolio of your work.

"I took a similar class at my old school. A lot of my work is online, so I was able to show my skills. I'm Benjamin Hopkins, by the way." He held out his hand, and I hesitantly slipped mine into it. An electrical current shot between us. He jumped, so I knew he felt it too.

"Damn, sorry about that. Static."

"I'm Davis. Er, Spencer Davis." Who stutters their own name? Ugh.

"It's nice to meet you, Davis Spencer Davis."

I giggled. Giggled! Like some giggly, gaggly girl. That was so not me. I never giggled.

I withdrew my hand quickly and glanced toward the front of the class. All eyes were on me and Benjamin. At least, all the girls' eyes. The teacher looked none too pleased at the class's obvious fascination with the new student. The yummy new transfer student.

"Class!" Mr. Campbell barked. "Start on Lab Twelve.

Mr. Hopkins, you can join Ms. Davis, as her lab partner is absent today. You have twenty minutes, people. And Mr. Payne? I'm watching you."

Ryan tried to appear innocent, but Mr. Campbell knew better. All the teachers did. Ryan was in trouble so much, his mother took a job in the school library just so her commute would be shorter when the principal called her in. Ryan was technically "gifted" but too easily distracted. He used his intelligence to disrupt class, and lab time was his favorite. Ryan was more of an evil genius and would make a wonderful nemesis for an aspiring superhero.

I turned my attention back to my hot lab partner, Benjamin. Can I just say again how much I love flu season?

Instead of gaping at my new partner, I opened the cabinet under the countertop and grabbed various items we would need for our experiment. Benjamin opened his lab book to our assignment and whistled low.

"Sorry your regular lab partner is gone and you're stuck with me, Spencer. I'm not very good at chemistry." He gave me a charming smile that caused the corners of his eyes to crinkle.

"No problem. Shannon is always gone." Actually, Shannon is never gone, and she's healthy as a horse. This was the first time I think she'd missed a day of school in all the years I'd known her. She prided herself on getting the perfect attendance award.

Benjamin reviewed the experiment and shook his head as though he didn't understand what to do next. He fumbled around, trying to light the Bunsen burner. Something wasn't right here. This was advanced chemistry. No way he was as incompetent as he seemed. Suddenly it dawned on me.

"So, what sport do you play, Benjamin?"

"Soccer," he replied, not taking his eyes off his task.

"And I take it you're very good at soccer?"

He looked at me and smiled. "I hold my own." Which meant he was a soccer god.

"Uh-huh, and let me guess, your last lab partner did all the work because she valued your soccer skills so highly?" I crossed my arms in front of me and pursed my lips.

He jerked his head up in surprise and, noting my stance, slowly broke into a genuine smile. "You're smart."

"Yeah," I leaned forward to whisper. "Just so you know, I'm not fooled by your 'little boy lost' routine, but I *am* used to doing the experiments by myself, so I guess you're off the hook today."

"Really? Why?"

"Turn your head to the right."

He looked past me. The windows against the wall faced the athletic field. A game of soccer was in progress, and some of the guys had stripped off their shirts.

"Your lab partner pays more attention to the scrimmages

than the experiments?" he deduced, amusement in his voice as he watched the field.

"Let's just say Shannon is a huge fan of all sports. Especially when they play skins versus shirts."

Benjamin chuckled and continued to watch the game. I managed to start the Bunsen burner with no problem and began measuring and pouring solutions.

"You're not a big soccer fan, Spencer?"

I slipped on a pair of safety glasses and slowly poured some solution into the beaker. "It's all right. I go to the games. Support the team, you know. Go Beavers. Go Pirates. Go Pirating Beavers."

He turned back toward me, laughing, and I felt a warm sensation creep up my neck. *Please don't blush. Not now.*

"Hey, you're blushing!"

Busted.

I tried to play it cool. "Curse of fair skin. If you're a fan of red, you should see me in the summer when I forget to put on sunscreen."

After the solution was poured to exact measurements, I opened my folder and gave him a copy of the lab questions, already answered.

"Hey, you didn't even know I'd be here today." He seemed surprised, yet accepting, that someone did his work for him.

"Dude, I already told you. I'm used to doing the experiments alone. Why mess with a system that works?"

I wondered if he'd hand back the questions and insist on doing the work himself, but he didn't. I got the impression I wasn't the first girl to do his homework. I bet he never had to do his own work.

He reviewed the questions, tucked them into his folder, and then looked at me.

"I think I like you, Davis Spencer Davis."

I tried not to blush again but felt the heat rising. "Good thing, 'cause according to your schedule, we have two classes together."

I said it gruffly, embarrassed that his confession of liking me caused such an obvious reaction. Inside, my stomach did loop-de-loops, and my heart beat like a jackhammer. Surely he could hear it, sitting right next to me.

"Lucky me," he responded.

Did that mean he *wanted* to see me two times a day? Or did he just figure I wouldn't mind letting him copy my work in all the classes and he'd have half the homework load? I prayed it was the first one and not the latter.

"Pass me that powder. We have to add it to the solution now that it's boiling."

The rest of class went quickly, with me concentrating

hard on not focusing on Benjamin. He was a surprisingly helpful lab partner, for all his bluster about being incompetent. We made a good team. Sort of like a surgeon and nurse during an operation. I asked for something, and he gave it to me. Not a totally auspicious beginning, but relationships had been built on less.

Hadn't Justin and Morgan hooked up at a party where his band played after she'd puked on his favorite shoes? Sometimes love conquered all. At least it did when they were on-again.

But I had destiny on my side. Love would come along. It had to.

Next period I sat next to Alyssa. The only free spot was across the room, so Benjamin wasn't within chatting distance. Which ended up being a good thing, because Alyssa wouldn't shut up about him.

"Have you ever seen such muscles on a teenage boy before?" She sighed heavily, completely ignoring the blank sketchbook in front of her.

"You're supposed to be drawing." I pointed to the fruit bowl on the artfully draped fabric tablecloth.

She completely ignored me, chewing the end of her charcoal pencil. "I hear he plays soccer. Was the MVP for his team last year. I wonder why he transferred to May Valley?"

"Maybe his family moved?"

"Nah, he could still drive to his old school. River View isn't that far away. It's got to be something else."

"Obsessed much?"

"There are few things in life as fine-looking to obsess over," she retorted.

"Tell the Stalker Society I said hello."

"Puh-lease, you're not the least bit attracted to him?"

I finally took my eyes off the project to look over at Benjamin. He sat slightly in front of me, so I checked out his sketching. Not bad. Needed to work on his draping, but the play of light and dark was intriguing. As if sensing me, he looked over his shoulder and caught me staring. To save face, I flipped my poster-size sketchbook around so he could see my sketch, as though I was really just interested in his artwork.

He nodded his head and mouthed the word *nice*, then turned back to his sketchbook. He scooted his stool to the side so I had a better view of his work, looking at me expectantly. I gave him the thumbs-up sign, and he grinned.

"What was that?" Alyssa watched our exchange and whispered frantically after Benjamin turned his attention back to his sketching.

"What was what?" I tried to act nonchalant.

"Don't give me that, Spencer Davis. You're holding out on me. You *know* him."

"Hardly. He was my lab partner in chemistry. That's all."

She gasped. "Why didn't you tell me?! I've been blathering about him for the last twenty minutes, and you actually talked to him. What's he like? What did he say? Spill it."

So I was forced to relive my conversation with Benjamin, but I omitted a few details. Like when he said he liked me and felt lucky to have me in two classes. I didn't want to share so much with Alyssa. I wanted to hide my new and unexplored feelings about him. Besides, Alyssa was like a shark. Spill one wrong detail, and you might as well drop chum in the water.

I admitted that he was hot. To not say that was tantamount to saying I was half in love with him. What with the whole "the lady doth protest too much" angle.

Final bell rang, and I slowly gathered up my supplies. Alyssa was packed and ready to go before I'd even closed my portfolio, sighing while shifting her weight from foot to foot.

"Hurry up," she hissed, casting furtive glances in Benjamin's direction. "I want an introduction."

Which was the sole reason I was dawdling. I wanted to keep Benjamin all to myself. At least for the first day. I'd introduce them on Monday. But right now it felt special, our introduction and his acknowledgment of me in class. Something I had attained that no other girl had accomplished yet. I wanted to savor the sensation a little bit longer.

In walked Shelby Grant. What was she doing here? She doesn't even take art. She made a beeline straight to Benjamin, stuck out her hand, and introduced herself. She flashed her diamond tennis bracelet as she coyly tucked a strand of perfectly foiled hair behind one ear. Her French-manicured fingers twisted the lock as she chatted with him, batting her lush lashes and giggling at whatever he had to say. It had taken her all of two hours to decide she wanted Benjamin, and she wasted no time in the pursuit.

What. A. Bitch.

I stuffed the rest of my art supplies in my bag and hurried toward the door, Alyssa now practically running to keep up.

"Can you believe her nerve?" Alyssa complained as we dodged students to get to our lockers.

"Nothing Shelby does surprises me anymore." I tried to sound apathetic, but the words choked in my throat. Shelby wanted Benjamin. What chance did I have against the richest, prettiest, most popular girl in school?

"She is the meanest, nastiest, bitchiest girl in school. What would Benjamin possibly see in her?" Alyssa contemplated. "She'll eat him alive. We've gotta save him."

"What?!"

"Yeah, it's our duty as May Valley students to protect transfers from narcissistic nut jobs. And Shelby is nothing

Serena Robar

if not that. Could there be a bigger drama queen in all the state?"

Alyssa had a point. Shelby loved romantic drama. She couldn't stand it when things weren't stirred up all around her, making her the center of attention. She would suck Benjamin into that ego vortex and crucify him.

Rumor had it her last boyfriend tried to dump her and she went psycho on his ass. He'd moved to Florida. Probably trying to get as far away from her as possible, though that could be neither confirmed nor denied.

No, Benjamin didn't need that kind of hassle. Maybe Alyssa had a point.

"I'm listening."

"You already know him. You share classes with him. Maybe you could share little tidbits of information that show Shelby's true colors."

"You want me to make up mean things about Shelby?"

"Dude, you don't have to make up mean things about her. She is evil personified. Last year she accused Mr. Minn of sexual harassment after he sent her home to change because her dress was too short. She was totally dressed the ho, and she got him *fired*."

"I thought he got fired for drinking during class."

She snorted. "I heard it was Shelby."

"I think your hatred for Shelby might be coloring your judgment."

"Oh, really." She folded her arms across her chest, then mimicked in a shrill, high voice, "'You can stop jiggling now.'"

I slammed my locker harder than I intended when Alyssa reminded me of that fateful day in gym. Shelby was mean and evil. Benjamin deserved better. Someone like me.

"Okay, I'm in. What's the plan?"

"Not here. Too many ears. We'll figure it out tonight at your house." Together we trudged to meet the Crew. Best friends, coconspirators and secret adversaries for Benjamin's affection. It could get complicated.

After school on Fridays, the Crew hung in the commons to discuss our weekend gaming plans (Guitar Hero, anyone?), and today was no different. When we arrived, Morgan and Justin were being civil, and I knew that by the end of the weekend, they would be a couple again. Unless Justin did something stupid. Like Shelby Grant. But that seemed unlikely now that Benjamin was in the picture.

Sydney walked by and called out, "See ya tonight, Zach."

Which immediately started the Alyssa inquisition. "Are you going out with Sydney Porter?"

Zach shrugged, a guarantee that Alyssa would push for more details.

"Is it a date? Where are you going? I want dirt."

"Sheesh, let the man breathe." Justin came to the rescue, sort of. "I'm sure our man Zach will give us all the naked details on Sunday, right?"

Zach blushed to the roots of his hair, and I empathized with him. Like me, Zach couldn't hide his embarrassment either.

"Not if I hit that first," Ryan joked, but there was an edge to his voice.

"Okay, you jackals, here's the story." Zach leaned in, and the entire Crew moved forward in anticipation. Zachary took a deep breath. "It's none of your business."

We groaned at being suckered. I should have known Zach wasn't going to give up any details. That wasn't his style. He was a gentleman—something Justin and Ryan just couldn't comprehend. However, I knew something else about Zach. What he wouldn't tell the group, he would tell one-on-one to the right person (that person being me).

"Whose turn is it?" Morgan asked over the din of the Crew all talking at once.

"I think it's Alyssa's turn."

"No way, we've banned Alyssa's on weekends, remember?" I had to speak up. *You big girl, you like food.* I shuddered.

"Then it's Ryan's turn."

"Yeah, buddy!" Justin and Ryan high-fived each other.

"Same time as always?" Ryan asked the group. We nodded.

"Great, I'll make sure the controllers are charged." We all heartily agreed, since the last time we were at Ryan's, two of his wireless controllers died and he didn't have any batteries. "And then your asses are mine, especially yours, Hobbs. Payback's a bitch."

"Bring it on," Alyssa trash-talked him right back. She was one of the best Guitar Hero players at the school. Which was funny, considering she played the violin and piano. It bothered Ryan to no end that our last session had ended with Alyssa getting five stars on Expert.

We disbanded, knowing we'd see each other on Sunday and perhaps run into one another at a party somewhere. I wasn't much of a party gal, so I was the one they entertained between sets with their weekend exploits.

Alyssa had piano lessons, then was coming to my house after dinner, so I needed to catch a ride with someone.

"Hey, Zach, can I get a ride home?"

Ryan opened his mouth as he started to mime riding a horse. It didn't take rocket science to figure out the sexual pun Ryan was trying to illustrate.

"Put a cork in it, Payne," I said, kicking myself for setting up the joke so effortlessly.

Ryan smiled and continued to "ride the horse" while slapping its imaginary flanks, silent as the grave.

"Sure." Zach laughed at Ryan and made his hand into a gun, pulling the trigger to put the "horse" down. Ryan stopped in midslap, dropping his hands and stating with dramatic sadness, "Aww, you shot my pony."

chapter

8

"Milady." Zach held open the car door for me with a slightly geeky flourish, but it was kind of cute when Zach did it. Once inside, I looked around the gray fabric interior and noted how tidy everything was. It didn't smell like week-old fast food, and he even had a small trash bag attached to the dash. Zach took great care of his things. We could all take a lesson from Zachary Thames.

"So," I said, once he was settled in the driver's seat and had started the car.

"So what?"

"So, what's new?" I tried to be casual, but I really wanted the scoop on him and Sydney.

He laughed. "God, you suck at subtle."

I grinned. Yeah, it really wasn't my forte.

"Well, then, fess up. What's the deal? Are you and Sydney dating? Is love in the air?"

Zach's expression went somber. Suddenly the mood in the car changed from lighthearted banter to serious discussion. Now I was more than curious, I was concerned.

"It's complicated," Zach finally admitted, brow furrowed.

"Complicated how?"

"You know. Just complicated."

I so didn't know.

"Well, let's uncomplicate things. Do you like her?"

He shrugged. "She's okay."

"Does she like you?"

He shrugged again. "She seems to."

God, is there anything more exasperating on the planet than trying to pry information out of a man? I don't think so.

"Have you kissed her?"

Not sure why that question popped out of my mouth. I guess it was the quickest way to figure out someone's intentions. If they put their tongue in your mouth, it was a pretty good sign that they were into you. At least, that was my working thesis, sadly untested.

"What if I did? Would that matter to you?"

I sighed dramatically. "Of course it would. I would be devastated and crushed that you kissed Sydney and *didn't tell me about it immediately.*" I poked him playfully. "You know I'd tell you."

"That you kissed Sydney?" he asked eagerly. "If you let me watch, I'd consider it my early Christmas present."

"Oh, ha, ha. Somewhere, Ryan's head is exploding." Before he could answer, I added, "and I'd make you download it off the Internet for a fee, just like everybody else."

We both laughed, any awkwardness evaporating away.

Zach decided to change the subject from his Sydney entanglement, and I let him. He obviously wasn't ready to talk about his relationship with her, and that was okay. I'd laid the groundwork, and when he was ready to talk, I would be the one he would go to.

"Alyssa says you know the new transfer student."

I coughed, careful to keep my voice neutral. "I think 'know' is a bit strong. We were lab partners in chemistry."

"Ah, so you haven't ripped your clothes off and begged him to be your baby daddy?"

"That would be a safe assumption," I replied drily.

Although I wondered how long it would take Alyssa to go that route.

"All the girls are flipping over him. They think he's so *hot*." He raised his voice to a falsetto, impersonating a love-struck girl perfectly.

I batted my eyelashes furiously in his direction. "Dreamy. He's just dreamy." I laughed until I realized that Zach hadn't joined in. "What?"

"Do you think he's hot?"

"I said *dreamy*." I tried to joke him out of his query.

"Whatever. Do you?"

When had this stopped being a joke?

"I don't know. I guess he's hot. I hadn't really thought about it. Not really my type."

I felt my face burn red at the outright lie. Would Zach notice?

Zach seemed to relax. "Yeah, he really isn't your type."

"What's that supposed to mean?"

"Nothing, I'm just agreeing with you. I can't really see you with a pretty-boy jock."

And why not? I wanted to yell. *Don't you think a pretty-boy jock could possibly find me attractive enough to date?* I knew I wasn't some anorexic cheerleader with bleached blond hair, but I wasn't exactly head of the Alpo line either.

I turned my head to stare out the window, not willing to speak for fear of what I might say.

Zach didn't seem to notice. He started to hum along with the radio, suddenly in a good mood. I wanted to slug him.

We pulled up to my house and I jumped out of his car quickly, muttering a thanks as I slammed the door. He unrolled his window and shouted, "See you Sunday." Instead of affirming our time at Ryan's, I ignored him. If he asked about it later, I would say I didn't hear him. I just didn't trust myself to say something I wouldn't regret later.

"I'm home," I called out once inside, dropping my backpack and purse onto the floor of the foyer.

No answer.

I tossed my coat onto the coat rack (it slid past the other coats and landed in a heap on the floor, but I ignored it) and made my way to the kitchen. I needed chocolate and I needed it now. Our pantry was always stocked with nutritious treats like dried pineapple chunks and trail mix, but I ignored the pantry and went straight to the tool drawer, where Dad kept his stash of sweet, sugary goodness. This was no time for all-natural sugar; I needed a Kit Kat bar. Now.

I slid open the drawer as far as it would go and cheered inwardly when I saw that Dad had restocked recently. I grabbed the familiar red wrapper and slid the drawer closed.

Serena Robar

"Busted!"

I shrieked while my sister laughed from the stairs.

"You scared the crap out of me. What are you doing home, anyway?"

She took a bite of the apple she had in her hand (she was so good about her eating, it made me sick) and replied, mouth full, "Thanksgiving break."

"Oh." *Well, duh.* I couldn't think of anything else to add, so I tore open my candy bar and snapped off a section. "Mazel tov." I saluted her with it and took a healthy bite. Yummy.

"So what happened at school today?" She slid onto the bar stool at the end of the island by the tool drawer.

"Nothing," I mumbled, chocolate coating my mouth.

"Uh-huh, you went straight for Dad's stash. Something happened."

I watched her munch quietly on her apple, big blue eyes staring at me. My sister was nineteen, petite, and perfectly proportioned. If she hadn't possessed the same wild, curly hair as I did, I would doubt we were related. Unlike me, however, she took the time to tame it into a gorgeous fall of waves, while I still used the ol' ponytail standby. That was our personalities in a nutshell. She was disciplined and I was, well, not.

"Nothing. Zach just pissed me off."

"Lovers' quarrel?"

"Hardly." I didn't even try to defend our relationship anymore. Heidi had been teasing me about Zach for years. She was convinced we were secret boyfriend and girlfriend. She couldn't seem to grasp the concept of platonic friendship between the male and female genders.

"Did he kiss you? Not kiss you? Slap your ass? Not slap your ass? What?"

"Enough already. He just said something that hurt my feelings. I doubt he even knew he did it."

"Oh, well, that sucks. What did he say?"

"It doesn't matter."

"Sure it does, you're obviously upset. I mean, you've inhaled that Kit Kat and are thinking of diving back into the drawer for another."

I moved my hand away from the drawer quickly, feeling guilty that she could read me so well.

"He said I wasn't the pretty-boy jock type."

She blinked at me once. Twice. "And you think you are because . . ."

"I didn't say I was. But it would be nice to think that my friends would be supportive enough to say I could be anyone's type. That I was worthy, you know? Of anyone's attention."

"Okay, who's the boy?"

"What boy?"

"You know what I mean. There *is* a boy. A pretty jock boy? It's not Ryan, is it?"

"No, it's not Ryan." We both shuddered. "There's a new guy at school. He's a transfer student. Some soccer star from River View. We have a couple of classes together. End of story."

She analyzed me a moment, thoughtfully chewing her apple.

"You *like* this guy."

I didn't try to deny it.

"You really, really like this guy," she said, her voice full of awe. "You never fall for anybody, and you've fallen for this guy. Wow."

She rushed to the window to peek outside.

"What are you doing?"

"Checking for locusts or a plague. You liking some guy is like one of the seven signs of the apocalypse."

"Not helping." I yanked open the tool drawer for another candy bar. Screw it.

She came over and put her hand over mine, effectively blocking my goal.

"That is not going to solve anything."

"Wanna bet?" I pouted, trying to push past her.

"It will make you depressed and mopey exactly thirty seconds after you scarf one down."

She was right, of course, but I didn't need *her* telling me how to live my life or eat my food. Heidi never had guy problems, and she certainly didn't have any chocolate-binge-eating issues. She was just like Mom, with her healthy eating and exercising regularly. I liked Dad's approach: Pretend you're working out when you're really reading a paper in the hammock out back, and hide all the sweets you can.

"What are you doing here?" I demanded, annoyed that she was right and how that always reduced me to being a sullen baby within seconds. She might go to school two hundred miles away, but it didn't change our dynamic. I was still the bratty younger sister, and she was still the bossy older one.

"Look, I'm not here to harass you. As a matter of fact, just the opposite. I want to help."

"Help? How?" Beware of older sisters bearing gifts.

"I know how tough it's got to be for you right now. What with your sixteenth birthday and all." She nodded her head knowingly. The Pill. Of course she knew that. She'd gone through the same thing at my age. Except she didn't have an older sister to prepare her.

"It totally tripped me up too. But I can help. Your body is going all crazy with hormones, and you're trying to pick out the right guy to be your first time."

"Really? You think that's what's happening? Seriously?"

Sarcasm dripped from every syllable of my speech. "Just a molten cauldron of screaming libido. That's me."

She looked sheepish and shrugged. "Well, it was like that for me. You've always been way more disciplined about guys than I ever was."

Disciplined? Me? Didn't she just witness the Kit Kat scarfing? She had to be kidding.

"Look, you're the reasonable one," she continued. I tried to object, but she cut me off. "Don't get your panties in a twist. I don't mean reasonable in a bad way. Trust me, I wish I possessed a quarter of your practicality. I think of all the bad decisions I made because I wasn't ready. I wasn't there, you know? Mentally. You've always been very self-aware, and I admire that, I really do. You won't rush off and do something stupid just because you can. You'll be smart about your choices. I wish I had that kind of common sense."

I thought about what she said. Was I really the reserved, smart one, or was I the timid, too-afraid-to-take-what-I-wanted one? Was I waiting for the "right" person, or was I too afraid to go for it and risk rejection?

Justin said I was the type of girl who needed love for her first time. I'd always thought my first time would be with someone I loved, but Alyssa seemed to think that was an antiquated concept. She was betting her first time on an experienced guy who she knew and was attracted to, but not one she wanted a relationship with beyond the first dirty deed.

I sighed heavily.

"Thanks, Heidi, but I think you may be a bit premature on the whole 'first time' thing. Just because this new guy has captured my interest, that doesn't mean anything more than he has my attention. I doubt he even sees me in that way. And just because I can have sex safely doesn't mean I'm ready to have it at all."

Lightning would surely strike me dead at that outrageous lie.

She nodded, finishing her apple and chucking it into the garbage can. "See, you're so much more mature than I was at your age. Than anyone I knew then. But if you want to talk, I'm here. At least until Thanksgiving." She smirked in my direction before ambling away. Her narrow hips swayed with each step, and her dark brown hair bounced lightly around her shoulders.

I stared at the empty corridor for several minutes, thinking about my sister and what her mistakes might have been. She probably did something stupid like hooking up with a guy like Ryan, assuming he would call her the next day, and when he didn't she was mortified, ashamed, and probably pissed off. I certainly would be, but like she said, I wouldn't be with someone like Ryan. At least, I felt pretty sure I wouldn't.

I thought of Justin's cocky grin. I had considered that option, but only after it was presented to me. Would I be equally strong if he hadn't taken no for an answer and poured on the charm? What if he pursued me with the same single-minded determination he showed when someone told him he couldn't do something? He'd learned how to play the drums in a single summer because someone said he couldn't. I shivered. No, as handsome as Justin was, it wasn't his face that kept returning to my memories. I saw green eyes and a strong jaw. I smelled the ocean breeze. I thought of Benjamin.

chapter 9

Alyssa arrived around seven in the evening. She'd grabbed supper at her house and then came over to watch the new season of DVDs waiting on the table. We carried her sleeping bag upstairs to my room, since we'd decided an all-nighter was in order so we could watch as many episodes as possible.

We dumped her duffel, pillow, and bag at the end of my bed. She threw herself onto my comforter and stretched. She'd changed into sweats and a tee, the perfect sleepwear for insomniacs hooked on sitcoms.

"I'm sooo glad it's the weekend," she declared, arms

stretched over her head. Her shirt rode up, revealing a flat stomach and tanned skin. I double-checked my shirt to make sure it hadn't crept up, and sighed wistfully.

"So where are they?" she asked.

"Where are . . . ? Oh, the pills. They're on my dresser." I pointed toward them.

She jumped up and grabbed the bag. I hadn't looked at them since the first day I got them. They weren't all that new or intriguing to me, but Alyssa thought they were fascinating.

"They're so tiny," she said in awe, holding open the compact. "Hard to believe something that small can be effective, huh?"

"Only abstinence is one hundred percent effective," I parroted my mother. When I realized what I'd done, I clamped my hand over my mouth, horrified.

She grinned. "Thank you, Mrs. Davis."

"See what one unguarded moment and years of brainwashing will do to a person?"

She laughed, leaned over the edge of the bed, and pulled a small notebook from her duffel. The faces of two sweet kittens were emblazoned on the front cover.

"What's that?"

"My goal planner."

"Dear Lord, no!" I made a grab for it and pried it from her

fingers. "You can't be serious!" She struggled to take it back from me, but I flipped it open.

"Step one: Make a list of possible candidates, include pros and cons." And she'd listed seven guys, and under each guy's name was a pro and con list. Some of the names I expected, such as Ryan Payne and Benjamin Hopkins, but there was one name that I wasn't expecting. At all.

"Zachary Thames?!"

She took advantage of my momentary shock and snatched the notebook from my hand. She shoved it back into her duffel and zipped it up tight.

"Tell me I didn't just see Zach on your list of possible first time candidates."

"What's wrong with Zach?"

"Well, nothing. Zach is great, but to make him your first? In what world does that make sense?" I didn't know why I was so annoyed that she would consider Zach. If I was being rational—which I wasn't, much to my dismay—Zach made a lot of sense. He was sweet, gentle, and funny, and he would be properly awed by the honor she was granting him. But Zach as a *one-night-stand* possibility? I so didn't get it.

"I happen to think Zach is kind of sexy in that geek hot sort of way," Alyssa continued. "And why should you care anyway? It's not like you're interested in him. Or are you?"

Interested in Zach? Hardly. I mean, I agreed with the geek hot assessment, and I wasn't unaware of his broadening shoulders and mischievous grin. He made me laugh, and I felt totally comfortable around him, but the thought of kissing Zach freaked me out. "You don't get that brotherly vibe from him? I just don't equate Zach with passion, you know?"

She shrugged. "You never know until you try. I'm not crossing him off the list until I know for sure, one way or another."

I felt that tinge of apprehension I got whenever Alyssa came up with one of her experiments. "What gets someone crossed off the list, exactly?"

She took my question seriously—I could tell by the expression on her face. Methodical reasoning made her a great student, but it was disconcerting to see her apply those skills to real life.

Ignoring my question, she said, "I think Zach has tingle possibilities."

I was afraid to ask but did anyway. "Exactly what are tingle possibilities?"

She sat up and rubbed her arms, as though she were cold. I waited patiently, knowing she would reveal all as soon as she organized the "tingle" list. I didn't have long to wait.

"What I want from my first time is a guy who makes me

feel tingly. And not just down there. I want my stomach to do a little flip when he stands too close or when he touches my shoulder. I want to feel like leaning into him when he's standing by my side. Of course, I want his kisses to curl my toes." She stared into space, lost in these thoughts, talking as though I wasn't even there. "I want all the physical excitement but not all the emotional entanglements."

"You can't possibly believe that Zach would make a good one-night stand." Had she met the boy? Seriously. Zach was a hopeless romantic through and through. He was anonymous love poems and surprise bouquets of flowers. He was not a "wham, bam, thank you, ma'am" kind of guy.

"Yeah, well, that is why Zach is on the bottom of the list and his romantic side is listed in the cons column. I like that I've known Zach forever, and I feel comfortable around him, but I do worry he would read more into sex than I do."

I blew out the breath that I hadn't realized I was holding. Good, then. Zach wasn't a top candidate for her ridiculous scheme. I felt much better.

"That's why Benjamin made the top of my list."

That so did not make me feel better.

"He's new, so we don't have any friendship history. He's hot, so you know he's got experience, so probably the event wouldn't suck, and I do get totally tingly whenever he's near."

"You've been near him once." It was up to me to be the voice of reason.

"Exactly. And it was a very powerful impression he made on me. Zowee." She rubbed at the goose bumps on her arms again. I was attracted to Benjamin too, and I didn't remember getting goose bumps. But did that really matter in the scheme of things? One person's goose bumps were another person's heart palpitations.

"What will you do if Benjamin likes another girl?" I tried to be casual, busying myself by tidying my desk so she wouldn't think I was worried over her answer.

"I expect there to be competition. I mean, look at him. But I can offer him something those other girls won't consider: a no-strings-attached sexual liaison, where he will be encouraged to brag about his conquest to his friends."

"You have got to be kidding me. You *want* him to brag about it?"

She sighed deeply, as though she couldn't believe I was so thick as to not see the genius of her plan. "What has been my biggest social obstacle since we started high school?"

"Your mom?"

"Ha, ha. Besides her."

"The fact that you look like you're twelve?"

"Exactly! I don't see that changing overnight, and if I stay like this much longer, the only guys I will be able to attract are potential pedophiles. No, thank you. I need guys to start seeing me as a *woman*, a sexual being."

"And you think sleeping with Benjamin will open up the playing field once the school learns you are no longer a virgin."

"Dude," she said with a certain amount of desperation, "it couldn't hurt."

I silently appraised her, letting this crazy, mixed-up notion sink in. When had anyone ever referred to Alyssa in a sexual way? Even Ryan didn't make the raunchy sex jokes about her that he did with everyone else. I pursed my lips in reluctant acceptance. Alyssa looked liked a child, and therefore she was never thought of as anything other than a child. I mean, I saw her slutty side and knew what sort of depravity lurked in her heart. A getting laid to-do list? The girl was harboring some serious sexual issues. But how could I help? I didn't want her sleeping with Zach, and I sure as hell didn't want her sleeping with Benjamin, so how could I honestly give her the support she needed?

"Listen, I don't expect you to understand my situation. You've got more boobs than any girl has a right to own, and all the guys picture you naked, but I don't have those kind of, er, weapons at my disposal."

I laughed. "No one is undressing me with their eyes, Alyssa, I assure you."

She stared at me long and hard, until I started to feel a little uncomfortable. "You see what you want to see, but your perception of yourself is skewed. If I had your body, I wouldn't hide it under sweatshirts that were way too big for me. *I* would put the twins on display." She pointed toward my breasts.

I smiled at her joke but couldn't help being irked. I didn't have a warped view of my body. I saw it naked every day. I didn't need some hundred-pound stick who could wear anything and still look good tell me that my self-esteem had issues. I wasn't the one plotting a one-night stand, hoping the guy I chose would be pig enough to tell all his friends so I could finally feel like a woman.

I went into the bathroom to keep from venting on Alyssa. She didn't get how her comment made me feel. She knew me better than anyone else, but she was wrong about this. Dead wrong. And I needed a moment to compose myself.

After I splashed some water on my flushed face (I get pink when I'm angry, too), I took some deep breaths to calm down. Then I rejoined her in the bedroom. She was listening to her iPod, spinning the packet of pills over and over in her small hands. I didn't dare ask what she was thinking, but instead motioned for her to join me in the living room to watch our show.

We ordered pizza and continued with our marathon. My sister even hung out for an episode or two. Around one in the morning, both Alyssa's and my cell phones beeped. Our gasps were practically identical when we opened the picture that had been forwarded to us.

Morgan had taken a picture of thirteen boys, bare-assed and staggered down football bleachers, with MORGAN WILL YOU GO OUT WITH ME?, two letters per ass, painted on their buttocks. Justin was in front of the message, on bended knee, with a rose that had seen better days clenched between his teeth.

I tried to recognize the rest of the guys, but it was tough, because most had their faces turned away from the camera. I picked out Ryan looking over his shoulder and sticking out his tongue, hand clenched in the "rock on" sign.

Justin had managed to pull off the "over the top" requirement—I had to give him props for that. Morgan seemed suitably impressed, since she'd added "We R back 2gether" in the attached text message. I guess it takes all kinds of romance for all kinds of people. I was more of a candy-and-flowers sort of gal, but to each their own.

Alyssa whistled low, and I looked over her shoulder to see if her picture was clearer than mine.

"Check it out." She pointed to the figure next to Ryan. Though her screen was larger, the graininess had me straining to identify the guy she was pointing to. I gasped when I recognized the profile. Benjamin. First day in school and already in the thick of a party, being photographed with his ass hanging out.

I could never do that. Standing in my living room, dressed in a purple tank top and lounge pants on a Friday night, receiving party pics from someone else's phone sort of proved that point. My phone rang, and I practically dropped it.

Caller ID said it was Ryan.

"Hello?"

There was loud background noise and the bass of someone's stereo thumping into my ear. "Da-vis! Sweet pic, right? Did ya get it?" His dialogue sounded a bit slurred.

He'd been drinking. What a shocker. Not.

"I got it. My eyes may never be the same again."

Riots of laughter echoed into my ear, and I pulled the cell farther away to save my hearing.

"Nice ass, Ryan," Alyssa called over my shoulder.

"Is that 'lyssa? Put 'er on!"

I ignored his request and asked, "Who's driving tonight, Ryan?"

"Ah, Davis, are you worried 'bout me?"

Was there anything worse than a sentimental drunk?

"Seriously, Ryan, who are you with?"

"My main man, Benjie," he hollered, and a chorus of whooping followed.

"Let me talk to him."

I heard the phone jostle, and suddenly Benjamin's voice, sounding more sober, was on the line. "Hey, Davis Spencer Davis."

I smiled. "Friends don't let friends dial drunk, Benjamin. Or didn't they teach you that at River View?"

He laughed a little too loud, and I pulled the phone away from my ear again.

"It's all good."

"Have you been drinking too?"

"Just one beer, I promise."

"Isn't the point of a designated driver to not drink anything if they are driving?"

"I was just appointed the position, so I'm going to stop drinking, I swear."

Ryan broke into the conversation. "Davis, he must mean it, he's got his hand in the Boy Scout salute." More laughter and innuendos about hand gestures. Alyssa rolled her eyes and smiled.

"Thanks for the check-in, children," I said, shaking my

head. Even though they couldn't see me, the tone of my voice had the proper mixture of amusement and tolerance.

Ryan always called me from a party. Always. I didn't know why, because he didn't call Alyssa or anyone else. I guess he liked that I made sure he had a safe way to get home. Who knew why Ryan did anything.

"So whatcha wearing, Spence? Are ya naked?"

"Good night, Ryan."

"I bet it's some see-through number."

"Hanging up now, Ryan."

"Something with tassels."

I burst out laughing. Tassels?

"G'night, *boys*." I flipped my phone closed.

I was still smiling when I caught Alyssa staring at her cell picture.

"You really want your first time to be with one of those idiots?"

"Nah," she said firmly. "I definitely want it to be with that idiot." My mouth went dry when I realized she was pointing to Benjamin specifically.

chapter

10

So here's the deal.

Alyssa wanted Benjamin to be her first time, and I wanted him to be my first love. If getting naked with him happened as part of that plan, then I was willing to try it, except how could I pursue someone my best friend wanted for herself?

I lay awake thinking about this impossible situation with Alyssa's declaration still ringing in my head.

"He's the perfect one. Everyone else is off the list."

"Are you sure? What made you decide that?"

"The way he agreed to be the designated driver for Ryan

tonight. He was willing to forgo his drinking pleasure to be a good guy."

"You don't know if he's really going to do that. He was already drinking before they asked him. Maybe they'll end up at the bottom of a ravine tonight."

"Morbid much? Now you don't like Benjamin?"

I squirmed under her scrutiny. "I didn't say that. I don't *know* him. I just think you should at least talk to the guy and get to know him before crossing everyone off your list. It's too soon."

She pondered my statement a moment and then nodded in agreement. "You're right. I'm still fleshing out my pros and cons list. I'll give it another week, but then I have to choose."

"What's your hurry?"

"Winter Formal. That's the night. I need to get the right guy from my list to ask me to the dance, and then I'll be a virgin no longer."

Winter Formal was a little more than seven weeks away. Earlier today it seemed like forever until it would arrive, but for what Alyssa was now contemplating, it loomed right around the corner.

"That soon?" I squeaked.

"Dude, it's like *next year*." She laughed.

Technically she was correct. It was in January and therefore next year. It was like when you leave for Christmas break and say, "See ya next year," and everyone does a double take, 'cause saying it like that seems like you're leaving for a long time. It wasn't really a long time. It was just perception.

"We should do it together!"

"Thanks, but I think I want to try guys first."

"You're so funny I forgot to laugh. No, silly, I mean you and I should lose our virginity on the same night."

I shook my head. "There are some things that girls are expected to do together, like hit the bathroom, but I don't think there's a standing 'have sex for the first time on the same night as your best friend' rule. Unless there's been an update to the girls' rule book that I didn't get. Should I check my junk e-mail folder?"

"Can't you take anything seriously?" she complained, sitting back down on the floor and wiggling into her sleeping bag.

"No, because one of us must be comic relief. You get so intense about stuff, and I have to lighten you up. I am the yin to your yang. That's why we work."

"It gets so annoying some times." She punched her pillow to emphasize her point.

"Yeah, tell me about it." I arched an eyebrow at her before settling into my sleeping bag as well. I heard a pillow whiz through the air before hitting me in the head.

"Don't sabotage my efforts on this. Be neutral. Be Switzerland."

The least I could do was promise not to ruin her chances with Benjamin. I wasn't going to help them either, because I wanted him for myself, but I wouldn't torpedo a friend over a boy.

"Fine, I'll be Switzerland. Neither helping nor hindering your planned devirginization."

"Is that even a word?"

"It is now. Verb meaning the plan or plot to lose one's virginity by calculating the best boy to have a one-night stand with to get it over with already."

She giggled. "Think Webster's will add it?"

"If not, we'll send it to *The Colbert Report*. He coined the term 'truthiness'; maybe 'devirginization' is the next big thing."

"You're really weird sometimes—has anyone ever told you that?"

"Says the girl with a 'How to Get Laid the First Time by Winter Formal' notebook in her duffel."

"Touché."

"Go to bed already." I tried to sound sleepy but came across exasperated.

"Wow, you're cranky late at night. Maybe it's best if your first time isn't Winter Formal. No guy's gonna want to get close enough to poke the bear."

I threw the pillow back at her head.

"Hey!"

"Poke the bear. Jeez . . ."

We both laughed and then settled down for the night.

Winter Formal. Six weeks away. I listened to Alyssa's breathing, waiting for it to even out and prove she was asleep. I couldn't sleep now that I knew my best friend wanted to sleep with My Destiny.

What was I going to do? Should I confess that I, too, had feelings for Benjamin and we should draw straws for him? No, she'd probably suggest that neither of us was allowed to go for him, since we both liked him and it wouldn't be fair. How would I feel if he picked Alyssa over me? Could I handle it? I flipped onto my back and sighed.

This was so complicated. Everything seemed way easier before Benjamin arrived. Actually, everything seemed way easier before my doctor's appointment. I glared in the direction of the pill bag, silhouetted in the darkened room.

Slowly I crept out of my bed, stopping every few seconds to make sure Alyssa wouldn't wake up, and made my way toward the dresser. I picked up the bag, taking care not to crinkle the paper unnecessarily, and tiptoed with it to the bathroom. I put the lid down and sat on the toilet after turning on the light and locking the door.

I pulled out the compact and opened it. Winter Formal was only seven weeks away. What if that was really the night Benjamin and I confessed our love and consummated our relationship? Shouldn't I be prepared? Nervously, I ran a finger over the bubbled plastic that protected the pills.

Of course, I would demand that he wear a condom. After all, I knew I was clean, but Benjamin was sure to have had his share of sexual partners. My mother had drilled safe sex into my head since I'd foolishly asked where babies came from in the third grade. Condoms weren't foolproof. They could break. They could be defective or past their expiration date. Briefly I wondered if Bekka had used a condom on that fateful night and if she really wished her mother had taken her in to get the Pill when she turned sixteen.

God, was I really going to do this?

I stood up and filled a glass full of tap water. To take it or not to take it? I looked at myself in the mirror. Who would know if I started taking them? I had a three-month supply and a prescription waiting for me at the pharmacy. I could pick up more and my mother would never know. Of course, it probably didn't matter if she knew. I chewed on my lower lip.

I really didn't want my friends to know. If they knew, it would take less than a day for Ryan or someone to tease me about it in front of Benjamin, and then where would I be?

Dying of mortification? Expiring from embarrassment? No, if I was going to do this, it had to be in total secrecy.

I dialed the pack to day one and gently pushed down on the first pill. It popped into my hand with little fuss. There. It was out. It was so tiny. So *benign*. My hand shook, the tiny pill shivering in my sweaty palm.

To take it or not to take it? That was the question. The glass of water sat on the edge of the counter expectantly. *Just pop the pill into your mouth and take a sip of me*, it seemed to reason. *What could possibly go wrong? Just because you are being prepared and responsible doesn't mean you have to go all the way. Just do it. No big deal. No one has to know. Just you and me.*

Damn, that drinking glass was very persuasive.

Then, without any more hesitation, I popped the pill in my mouth and guzzled down the water, practically choking on it in my haste. Sputtering and trying to silence my cough after sending a pint of water down the wrong tube, I froze when I heard Alyssa call from the bedroom.

"Hey, are you all right?"

Crap! I'd woken her up. I'm such a freak.

"Yeah," I got out in a gravelly bark. "Just got up to use the bathroom and get a drink of water."

"You've been in there *forever*. What did you have for dinner?"

Great, she thought I was hanging out in the bathroom, stinking up the place with food-induced diarrhea. Nice.

"No, it's not that. Just sort of spaced out in here."

I shoved the bag of pills under the sink and hurried out of the bathroom. She shielded her eyes, a half smile on her face.

"Have I told you lately you're weird?"

"Not in the last half hour," I muttered under my breath as I dug back into my nest of covers.

"Good night?" she asked teasingly.

"Yeah, good night," I grumbled, and her light laughter filled the room.

chapter

11

Sunday approached with
lightning speed. I had all my homework done so I wouldn't
have it hanging over my head at Ryan's. Our afternoon
consisted of several bouts of Guitar Hero, co-op and head-
to-head. The boys usually wanted a good hour or so of Halo
(they mocked me because I got motion sickness playing
first-person shooters), and then we'd try whatever new
games we had.

Ryan's father ran several computer game companies.
He had a local office on the east side and a couple of out-
sourcing studios in China, so Ryan had the latest everything

in the gaming world. He also had a full-size basketball court and a swimming pool. Apparently, making games was a very good living. I wondered if Ryan's grandma ever nagged his dad as a boy to quit playing those silly games and do something constructive. Wouldn't that have been a hoot? Oh, the irony.

"Thanks for the late-night phone call, Ryan," I said when Alyssa and I walked through his front door.

He looked at us blankly.

"Never mind." I sighed.

Sometimes the guys teased me about never partying with them. Yeah, like I wanted to discover I couldn't remember who I'd talked to the next day after drinking myself into a stupor.

"Everyone here?"

"Yep. Help me carry some stuff downstairs."

Ryan's mother was in their mammoth kitchen, putting snacks onto the granite island for us to take downstairs.

"Hey, Mrs. P.!" we greeted her.

"Girls! How is everything?" She pulled out a half-full bag of pretzels from the pantry and tossed them toward Ryan as she continued to rummage.

"We're good. You don't have to go through all this trouble to feed us." I always felt a little bad about how often we descended on their house and ate like a plague of locusts.

"Please." She waved her hand. "You're doing me a favor. If someone doesn't eat this stuff, then I will. And no one wants that. Least of all my pants."

We chuckled. Not because what she said was so funny, though she was pretty amusing, but because Ryan's mom was still as slender and beautiful as any trophy wife half her age. Which was pretty cool, considering that she and Ryan's dad had been married for a good twenty years.

Ryan's dad was one of those nerds who made good during the technology boom, and his mother was the former Daffodil Queen of 1987. His father was sort of thin and gangly with a slight overbite, while his mom was a perfect size six, with a toned body, long golden hair, and impossibly flawless skin. Ryan got his looks from his mom and his intelligence from his dad. I figured there was a sociopath somewhere in the family tree who was the source for Ryans guilt-free rationale that his actions had no consequences.

Laden down with chips, cookies, donuts, and candy, we headed downstairs, where a bar held a large assortment of sodas. Ryan's dad had weekly game nights with his employees, so they always had plenty of munchies in the house, as well as every board game ever made. The best ones were from Germany, and it was great when Mr. Payne got a new shipment and taught us how to play them. Invariably there would

Serena Robar

be a disagreement about the rules, and we would all try to interpret the instructions, which were in German.

"Did your dad get any new games?" Alyssa asked as we got to the bottom of the secret staircase (it was hidden behind a bookcase—so cool).

"Nah, he's in China till Tuesday."

Ryan's entire basement was made for games. His father kept his personal office down there next to the recreation room. There was air hockey, a pool table, an arcade machine that housed more than a thousand classic video games, electronic darts, and in the bar two of those countertop coin-operated game machines usually seen in taverns. Except here they didn't cost anything to play.

We set up in the theater room, natch. Who else had a wall screen and projector hooked up to four different consoles with individualized recliner gaming chairs complete with cup holders?

"Yeah, buddy!" Justin called out as we unloaded the treats onto the bar. Morgan bounced over, glowing with rightness at being back together with Justin.

"Did you get my text Friday night?" She helped herself to a bag of Doritos.

"Yeah. You can tell it was taken in western Washington because all the butts were white," I joked, referring to the daily cloud cover.

I grabbed a handful of peanuts and popped them into my mouth. I caught a glimpse of Benjamin coming out of the movie room and started to choke.

Morgan pummeled on my back, while Alyssa grabbed a glass to fill with water. My eyes were watering when I finally cleared the airway. Couldn't I get through a day without choking since I'd met Ben? Had he seen me? How embarrassing!

Zach pounded down the stairs to join the Crew, and we assembled in our usual order. Alyssa and Ryan stood up in front while Morgan cuddled with Justin, and I found myself sitting between Zach and Benjamin.

It was time to start the first round of Guitar Hero. Alyssa played bass while Ryan played guitar during the warm-up match. They were the best players, and it was amazing to see their fingers work the buttons and strum the lever. Ryan was the king of the whammy bar.

"Hey," I said to Ben after I sat down. "What's a nice guy like you doing in a cutthroat Guitar Hero competition like this?"

He smiled sheepishly. "I invited myself. After seeing Ryan's setup yesterday and hearing how you guys play on Sundays, I had to check it out."

I nodded.

Ryan started the first song with a difficult riff before

Alyssa's bass notes flashed on the screen. Benjamin hooted and hollered his support to Ryan.

"So this display of blatant pandering will keep Ryan from releasing the hounds and kicking you out? Is that the plan?"

He laughed, and Cotton, Ryan's ten-pound Yorkshire terrier, barked in agreement.

"Apparently your butt kissing was effective." Cotton paused momentarily to look at us, then started to lick himself in an industrious show of personal grooming.

"Does Cotton mean anything, beside the obvious fluffy, white, absorbent ball?"

"His full name is Cotton McKnight."

"Cotton McKnight?"

"Yeah, he's named after one of the announcers in the *Dodgeball* movie."

The conversation died down as Alyssa joined the fray. The huge screen was alive with colors, both players looking at their side of the screen and feverishly following the strum strokes and button chords.

When the song ended, Alyssa had beaten Ryan by a single note.

"You've been practicing," she noted as she pulled the guitar strap over her head.

"And I still can't beat you." He turned his guitar over to Justin.

She smiled wickedly. "Not everyone can walk in the sun."

That comment made Ryan sling her over his shoulder and spin around the room. She squealed for him to stop. After each rotation, he'd tickle her. Finally, after many spins, he stumbled and they both tumbled to the ground.

Everyone laughed when Zach turned to Ben and said, "Usually you pay double for this kind of action."

I laughed harder, but Ben just stared at Zach blankly. I thought Zach was hysterical for quoting the movie *Dodgeball*, and I was surprised Benjamin didn't get the joke.

Zach cleared his throat awkwardly and jumped up to join Justin for the next round. I turned to Ben and said, "Not everyone gets Zach's humor."

"Oh, I got it. I just didn't think he was funny."

Uh, okay.

Alyssa, breathless from her helicopter ride, plopped down next to Benjamin. He congratulated her, and they chatted about which was easier, bass or guitar.

Zach and Justin started "Welcome to the Jungle," and I admired how they both got into the rhythm and swung the guitars around. They liked to stand next to the couches to interact with us. Justin even tried to play the guitar behind his head. He had a natural stage presence being the lead singer of his own band, but it really struck me how comfortable Zach looked on the stage, under the limelight. His large hands dwarfed the guitar neck as he feverishly pressed the buttons, banging his head to the beat with Justin. I smiled at the players, and Zach winked at me.

I was fanning myself in an exaggerated way, as though their playing was getting me hot, when Benjamin asked in my ear, "Do you play?"

Surprised, I turned my head quickly and found myself nose to nose with him. My stomach dropped and seemed to flip over—and then a sour chord yanked my attention back to the players. One of them had screwed up. I checked their meters and watched Justin activate Star Power. Zach had screwed up. Odd because he was usually the better player of the two.

He looked annoyed, and I smiled in sympathy. Surprisingly, he didn't smile back.

"So do you?" Ben repeated, pulling my attention away from Zach.

"Of course. I just don't play well. I feel pretty cocky if I can get five stars on Easy."

"At least you're good at chemistry. Speaking of which, did you check out the chapter questions? They looked crazy hard."

"I've already done them. They weren't too tough."

He shook his head in amazement. "I have to split early so I can do mine. In fact, I should leave now."

He started to stand, and I blurted out, "Just copy mine."

I couldn't believe I'd just offered to do his homework so he would stay next to me a little longer. How starved for attention was I?

His sexy smile made my heart race faster.

"Great. Then I can stay longer." He leaned closer and whispered, "With you."

He wanted to stay longer to be with me? My heart leaped around, dancing and singing, but I just gave him a small smile. I didn't want him to know how much his comment meant to me.

We played several more rounds of Guitar Hero. I made more mistakes than normal because I was nervous performing in front of Benjamin, but my friends cheered loudly for me all the same. Everyone except Zach, who seemed to have a bug up his butt about something.

We took a food break, and Alyssa pulled me aside.

"Did you just agree to do Benjamin's chemistry homework so he could stay longer?"

I stammered, unsure how to answer, when she threw her arms around my neck. "Thank you, thank you. I knew I could count on you to help me out."

She thought my homework offer had something to do with her stupid plan of getting Benjamin to sleep with her. Ugh.

I pulled out of her hug. "I'm Switzerland, remember?"

She winked knowingly. "Yeah, Switzerland. I get that." And she strolled toward Ben and Ryan, who were playing air hockey.

This so wasn't happening to me, was it?

Morgan offered me a soda at the bar, and I took a Mountain Dew. "Be careful with that one."

"With what one?" I stared at the can dubiously.

"Not the Dew, silly, with Ben. I hear he's got quite a reputation."

I looked over at the air hockey table, admiring the way Ben's strong arms defended the goal from Ryan's onslaught.

"Wow, gossip mill didn't take long, did it? Why are you warning me, anyway?"

She cocked her head to one side. "Because you blush every time he talks to you."

"I do not."

She quirked a pierced eyebrow at me.

"Really? Every time?"

"Don't worry. Only those who really know you would notice. Benjamin's a great guy, but he's not a one-girl kind of guy. Rumor has it he's all about sharing the wealth, so to speak."

As she spoke, Ben pulled Alyssa in front of him, put her hand over the air hockey mallet, and covered it with his. Ryan shot the puck at them, and he quickly dodged it, pulling Alyssa with him when he moved her hand. Ben's body pressed against Alyssa's back intimately as he "taught" her how to play the game.

I felt a flash of annoyance and then reluctant admiration. Alyssa played air hockey almost as well as she played Guitar Hero, and yet she'd managed to completely bamboozle Benjamin into full-body-contact instructions on how to block the puck. No one in the Crew was fooled by Alyssa's play-acting, but no one dared to "out" her. I knew the guys would later threaten Ben to behave around Alyssa and not try anything, because they all saw her as a precious porcelain doll, but maybe Ben liked the idea of the forbidden fruit?

That hardly furthered my cause, although Ben had singled me out to talk to and even wanted to stay to be with me instead of leave to do homework. Surely that said something about his feelings for me. Didn't it?

"I'm gonna bounce," Zach announced from behind me, pulling on his jacket.

"But it's early."

"Yeah, well, I need some air." He darted a look toward the air hockey table.

"Uh, okay, I guess." I didn't want Zach to leave, but he was in some kind of mood, so I wasn't sure I wanted to take the time to cajole him out of it either.

He started up the stairs, stopped, turned back toward me, and opened his mouth to say something. He seemed to decide against it and continued back up the stairs, out of sight.

What in the world was going on with Zach? And what was I going to do about Alyssa's goal to sleep with Ben? Morgan and Justin were kissing and cuddling by the arcade machine. With Zach's abrupt departure I felt very much like a third wheel.

chapter

12

Instead of hanging around downstairs, I pretended to get more snacks. I needed a few minutes to myself. Zach was mad, Benjamin was flirting with Alyssa, and suddenly I wanted to go home. I snuck upstairs.

"Who left?" Mrs. Payne popped her head around the kitchen corner.

"That was Zach."

"Oh," she said, surprised. "Early night for him, isn't it?"

I shrugged, sliding onto an island bar stool and popping some M&M's into my mouth.

"Trouble in paradise?" She wiped her hands with a dish-cloth and grabbed a few of the candy-coated chocolates.

"That's an oxymoron. Paradise by its very nature is un-troubled."

She whistled, opening one of the drawers to her right and pulling out snack-size Kit Kats, then dropping them into the candy dish. "That bad, huh?"

"Not bad, really, just confusing."

"So, typical teen stuff then, right?"

I laughed with her, snagging a Kit Kat. "Right."

"Oh, I know. Boys can be very confusing."

"What makes you think it's boy troubles?"

"Well, isn't it?"

"Could be," I hedged.

She tapped her temple. "Mom's intuition. Is that why Zach left early? You two have a spat?"

I swiveled back and forth on the barstool. "I have no idea why Zach left early. He's been in a mood lately."

"Hmm," she said, running a towel across the island's granite surface. "You know, I always thought you and Ryan would make a cute couple."

I almost choked on my Kit Kat.

She smiled at my distress. "I'm serious. You're very good for him. I know he's a wild child, but you would keep him grounded. And I've always thought he had a bit of a crush on you."

"No offense, Mrs. P., but Ryan can have any girl he wants." *And frequently does*, I added to myself. "He's not going to pick me. And second of all, we're just friends. Always have been. He doesn't see me that way. Trust me."

"You know, Spencer, I'm around you kids a lot. Here at the house and at school. I see things. Things that maybe you don't see because you're used to things being like they've always been. Ryan respects you and he values you.

"I love my son, but I'm not blind to his faults. He uses girls, terribly. It's the thing we fight about the most—well, besides when he's blowing up the chemistry lab—but he would never do that to you."

"He would never blow me up?" I joked.

She chuckled. "I couldn't promise you that, but he would never treat you poorly. He wouldn't use you."

I chewed on my Kit Kat thoughtfully. Mrs. P. was way off base about Ryan's affections. He was Ryan, after all. He had girls all the time. No way he'd give all that up for a fat virgin.

I changed the subject. "What do you think of Benjamin?"

She smiled warmly. "I think my son has found a partner in crime. Those two boys are going to give me a heart attack before graduation. I know it."

She said it with such affection that I didn't doubt for a moment that she loved her son deeply. She knew Ryan had his difficult moments, but she also had faith that he would grow out of it. His father put him to work at his company over the summer, and that seemed to curb some of his wicked ways. When he focused his creativity into making games, he didn't need to focus it on destruction and chaos. Probably a good thing.

"What are your plans for the holidays, Spencer? Family coming to visit?"

"Oh, yeah. It's our year to host, so my grandparents are coming up from Arizona, and my aunt and her family will be here as well. It'll be crazy."

"Your mother's a brave woman. Ryan's father always invites employees who have nowhere to go for the holidays to our house. I have the event catered, because I'm overrun with hungry men. Then they play games all night and the next day. Between you and me, I would rather let them have the holiday so I can escape to a spa."

We laughed.

Alyssa bounded up the stairs to join us.

"There you are! I wondered where you headed off—ah, Kit Kats. Now I get it."

She hopped up on the other bar stool and helped herself.

"How did your air hockey lesson go?" I arched an eyebrow at her.

She laughed at me. "I am a surprisingly quick study."

"Ha! You are a diabolical mastermind, and I can't help but be impressed with your acting abilities." I saluted her with a wafer bar.

"Alyssa? Diabolical?" Mrs. P. sounded unconvinced.

I looked over at Alyssa for permission to expose her plot, but Alyssa eagerly confessed.

"I pretended I didn't know how to play air hockey so Benjamin could educate me."

"He's a very hands-on teacher," I interjected. Uh-oh. Did that come out snotty? I looked at Alyssa, who was smiling like the cat who ate the canary. I hoped I didn't sound bitchy—or worse, jealous.

Mrs. Payne looked at Alyssa with new respect. "Who knew you had it in you, Hobbs?"

"Davis!" A shout came from downstairs. "You're up."

Alyssa and I hopped off the stools together.

"Duty calls." Mrs. Payne stepped aside so we could pass. "Just think about what I said, Spencer."

I turned back to her in confusion. Did she really think Ryan was going to date me? How crazy was that? She smiled at me the way a mother smiled at a daughter, which sort of

creeped me out. Sure I adored Mrs. P., but I almost felt like she was looking to arrange a marriage of convenience between me and Ryan. Sort of like my "stabilizing" influence would free her to quit working at the school and not have to worry about what Ryan was going to do next.

"What was that all about?" Alyssa asked when we started down the stairs. I grabbed her shoulder to stop her and whispered, "She thinks Ryan might have a thing for me and we would make a cute couple."

Alyssa didn't look surprised. "I'm not surprised."

"What are you talking about?! There's nothing between Ryan and me."

Alyssa looked down the stairs to make sure no one was coming to find us and whispered, "Spencer, he calls you when he's at parties. He doesn't call me, and he's always making sex jokes about you. Again, he doesn't do that with me."

My mouth opened and closed several times.

"I know you don't see it that way, and maybe I'm way off, but think about this: How many boy/girl friendships are like yours and Ryan's?"

She left me standing on the stairs. Was what she said true? Ryan did call me to check in at parties. He made sure I had a seat at the lunch table. He pilfered food from my tray (but to be fair, he did that to Alyssa, too, so it didn't really count).

Sure, he made sexual innuendos to me all the time, but I never thought of that as unusual. Ryan did that with plenty of girls, didn't he? Just not other girls in the Crew.

But if Ryan liked me, I mean *really* liked me, he would tell me, right? Justin only confessed his interest in me because he and Morgan were on a break, and I was "taking the Pill," and he thought we might have sex. Ryan had sex all the time with random women, but he'd never seriously made a pass at me.

On the other hand, as hot as Ryan was, he didn't make my blood race like Benjamin. Did Ryan feel more for me than friendship? I doubted it. Mrs. Payne just wanted to see something there that would help control her son. And Alyssa had such hang-ups about her sexual attractiveness that nothing she said could be taken as gospel.

"Da-vis! I'm aging here," Ryan yelled from the theater.

Could I go back in there and pretend that everything was normal and the same? *Was* everything normal and the same? Nothing had changed, really. Except now I would look at our relationship differently. Ryan wouldn't. He probably didn't even know what was going on, and I had no desire to make an ass of myself and even entertain the idea that he liked me. To harbor a secret affection for Ryan was emotional suicide.

Mrs. Payne had referred to Benjamin as Ryan's partner in crime. They were cut from the same cloth. So would I end

up doing Benjamin's homework forever while he called me at parties and I made sure he had a safe ride home—and he'd be hooking up with beautiful girls while I was stuck at home? It was a glum thought.

"Da-vis!"

"For the love of Pete, start a practice round or something," I hollered back. After a moment's pause, the game started up. I stood on the stairs, debating what to do, when the door to the theater room opened and closed. I was sure it was Alyssa coming to find me.

"Davis, Spencer Davis?" Benjamin said softly from the bottom of the stairs.

Ugh, not Ben, not now. I couldn't deal.

"You okay?" He sounded so sweet and caring.

"Yeah, fine. I'm just trying to remember if I, uh, took the trash out before I left home. My dad asked me to do it, and I didn't want to forget."

How lame was that excuse?

"So you're not on the stairwell all by yourself hoping I'd come up and join you?" he teased, making his way up the stairs to me.

I started to make a joke when I noticed his expression. It didn't look like he was teasing me. He looked kind of serious.

"A secret rendezvous in Ryan's staircase has long been a

dream of mine." I couldn't help the attempt at humor. It was my nature. After thinking about Ryan's attentions, I couldn't believe for a moment that Benjamin was into me. If I didn't have a low self-image before, this whole Ryan thing had certainly done it.

"Consider me your own personal genie of wish fulfillment."

I couldn't believe we were practically touching, my chest a hairsbreadth from his.

He reached out and palmed my cheek. "You're red. Are you all right?"

"Sunburn," I choked out, humor being my only defense against the onslaught of emotions I was feeling. He smelled so good and was standing so close. He was touching my face, and we were all alone in a dim stairwell.

"There's no sun today," he mentioned, stroking my jawline with his thumb.

"No?" I whispered, caught up in his green eyes. Was that a scar in his eyebrow? I reached up and touched it.

"What happened here?"

"Cleat to the head."

I nodded, amazed when his lips pressed onto mine, effectively quieting them. They were warm and soft, gentle but firm. How could his lips be firm and soft at the same time? I had no

idea, but it was true. I heard the door in the theater room open again, and Benjamin pulled back abruptly.

"Found her!" he called out, his voice cracking. He'd jumped three stairs away from me by then.

"It's your turn, Davis." Ryan looked exasperated. "Are you in or out?"

I stood undecided for a moment. Should I leave or should I stay? Benjamin wouldn't look at me. He was already headed down the rest of the stairs toward the theater.

"I'm in. Jeez, Ryan, don't get your panties in a twist."

I stepped down and brushed past him.

"I'll get your panties in a twist," he mocked when I stopped and turned to face him.

"I seriously doubt that."

He took a step back at my serious tone. I'm sure my expression was a sight to see. His gaze narrowed as he quickly covered the few feet between us. He got right in my face and spoke to me in a low voice.

"Name the time and the place, Davis, and I guarantee your panties will never be the same." My eyes widened in shock. "*Now* are you ready to play?"

I had a feeling he wasn't talking about games anymore. Benjamin had already left the vicinity. I tried to chuckle, but nothing would come out. Ryan was intense, serious—and I was completely speechless. Not to mention thrown for a loop.

What was going on all around me? What had changed? Was it the Pill? Did they really think I was a pill-pop away from promiscuity? And could I seriously blame the Pill for this one? Sure, I'd started taking it in case Benjamin and I developed a relationship, and by the soft kiss on the stairs I was hoping we were on our way. But Justin and now Ryan showing an interest? All this for a shot at my virgin status? It seemed pretty extreme.

Instead of answering him, I turned and walked woodenly into the theater to join the others. My head was spinning.

Ryan just didn't understand how girls thought of sex. He considered it a physical release. He didn't understand that most girls viewed sex differently. If someone like me offered him sex as a sign that she really liked him and that he was special enough for her to sleep with, he'd think of it like playing a pickup game of basketball. You got together with someone to shoot a few hoops, and when it was over, that was it. If you never played with them again, there were no hard feelings. It was just a shared physical experience. God, boys were so stupid.

The last thing I wanted to be was a notch on Ryan's bedpost, and despite what Mrs. Payne seemed to think, Ryan was not the kind of guy a girl like me could tame. I might be stabilizing (how horrid was that?), but I couldn't control

his behavior. Ryan needed a girl who could dish it out and match his sexual confidence. I could dish. I was hardly confident about sex.

I grabbed a guitar and picked an easy song I knew. I pushed the buttons on the guitar neck and strummed automatically. I really liked Benjamin. Would I sleep with him if I thought it would make him want to be my boyfriend? I watched him strum his guitar. He smiled and winked in my direction, then swung the guitar into Star Power mode. My stomach did a little somersault.

I matched his moves and thought about how well we played together. We seemed to be in perfect synch. His kiss on the stairs was very nice, if a bit brief. His lips had been oh so soft and unhurried. I shivered. Would everything with him be like that? Our song ended with both of us achieving perfect scores.

Alyssa challenged Justin once more, and then she had to leave. Since she was my ride, I left with her. We all made plans to meet on the following Sunday, even with Thanksgiving. It appeared that everyone was going to be in town. The guys and Morgan stayed to play Halo 3.

Back in the car, Alyssa sighed contentedly.

"What's up?"

"Nothing. Just thinking of Benjamin teaching me how to play air hockey."

I didn't reply. What *could* I say?

"Do you think he likes me?"

I worded my answer carefully. "Yes, I think he likes you." I felt bad telling her what she wanted to hear instead of telling her how I felt about Benjamin.

She giggled, which was unlike her.

"Okay, spill it."

"Spill what?" she asked.

"You've got information that you're not sharing and you're dying to tell someone, so spill it."

"Sometimes I hate that you know me so well."

"No, you don't. You love it, so fess up."

She grinned at me. "I think Benjamin likes me, too. He was very flirty as well as hands-on when he was showing me how to play."

"Flirty how, exactly?" I hoped my voice came across neutral.

She giggled again, and I ground my teeth.

"He told me I was giving him the yellow fever."

"What does that mean?"

She sighed in exasperation at my ignorance. "Yellow fever is Asian fever. You know, guys who dig Asian chicks say they have yellow fever."

"Really?" I'd never heard that, but then again, I wasn't Asian.

"So if he's flirting with me, then he probably doesn't see me as a little kid, ya know." She seemed so happy. "Now I need to make sure he knows I'm a woman."

"You're *not* a woman." I had to point that out.

Again she sighed in exasperation. If she kept this up, she was going to hyperventilate. "Okay, fine. Legally, *almost* a woman. Better?"

She continued to chat about Benjamin, but I stopped listening. I offered the occasional "uh-huh," and that seemed to satisfy her. I was thinking about my time on the stairs with Benjamin. Did it mean the same thing to him as it did to me? If he was telling Alyssa he had a fever for her, could he really mean what he said to me? Had my sarcastic remark about waiting for a secret rendezvous in the stairway been seen as a come-on? Had he thought, *Why not? She's offering?*

We arrived at my house, and I quickly escaped the car. Alyssa waved as she drove off. My once buoyant mood soured. Was Benjamin a player like Ryan? Zach couldn't seem to stand him, and that should have been an alarm, but I wasn't convinced. Benjamin seemed very sincere on the stairs. Was this desperate thinking on my part?

Maybe he was just flirting with Alyssa to make her feel special. Some guys were like that. Ryan flirted with everyone, but that was probably a bad example.

I felt my lips. They still tingled from his kiss. I really felt he and I were connected. My heart was telling me that Benjamin *liked* me. Wasn't that like a gut instinct?

I walked across the lawn to my front door. I'd play it cool on Monday and see how Benjamin acted. Let him take the lead. Then I'd know more. It was a short school week due to Thanksgiving, so if he wasn't interested in me, I wouldn't have to see him for several days. Long enough to get myself pulled together. But if he did like me, then those couple of days were going to seem like an eternity. God, this sucked.

Serena Robar

chapter 13

Monday morning I got up bright and early to do my hair. My sister promised to help, and we used all her anti-frizz stuff to keep the curls tame. I applied lip gloss and mascara, deciding against eye shadow, much to my sister's disappointment. She was treating me like her own personal Dress-Up Barbie and complained when I disagreed with some of her makeover suggestions. I even forwent my usual sweatshirt and instead put on a knit top. My sister assured me it minimized my bust and made my waist look smaller, but it showed cleavage, which made me nervous.

I stuck with jeans because I didn't want to make anyone

suspicious. Having my hair down was going to get me razzed enough. At least I could tell them my grandparents were coming into town today and my mom wanted me to look nice for them. No one needed to know I was really trying to look nice for Benjamin.

I put some eye drops in my purse for later. My contacts sometimes irritated my eyes, and if I didn't use some by lunch, it looked like I had pinkeye. Not my best look, to be sure.

Heidi even drove me to school, which showed how bored she was at home. I entered the school feeling self-conscious. I imagined there was a giant, flashing neon sign pointing me out. Fraud, fraud, fraud. I made it to my locker without any of the Crew seeing me. I worked the locker combination, and when it opened, I was assaulted with tons of mini Kit Kats falling from the top shelf. Taped to the front of the shelf was a badly rhymed poem, written on poster board.

Sometimes I'm quite sullen,
Other times I'm a bore,
I know hanging out with me
Can seem like a chore.

I'm glad you're willing,
To put up with my ways,

Cause being around you
Brightens my days.

This poem is dumb,
This poem is lame,
But you'll still forgive me,
You're a sweet, classy dame.

MP

I laughed. It was Zach, making up for his moodiness on Sunday. Gathering all the Kit Kats, I stuffed them into my backpack to keep them from spilling again. I pulled the poster down and folded it neatly, leaving it tucked in the bottom of my locker next to my other Zach notes.

MP stood for Mysterious Poet. Zach was the king of bad poetry. At least he hadn't chosen to honor me with another racy limerick. He liked to rhyme proper medical terms for sexual organs, which made for hilarious reading.

I strode down the hallway with a smile on my face. Zach could be so sweet. I forgot all about my dressier state when I ran into Benjamin, who let out a wolf whistle. I deflected the compliment with humor.

"You need to get out more."

"Only if you'll go with me." He grinned. "So, do you have something for me?"

I was momentarily confused. Did he want a hello kiss in the middle of the hallway? Was he serious?

"Huh?"

"Remember Sunday?"

I blinked several times in a row. Did he mean Sunday on the staircase?

"Chemistry homework?"

Ah, of course he wasn't referring to our kiss on the stairs. He wanted the homework I promised to do for him. He'd probably forgotten all about the kiss by now. Even though I'd gotten up hours early so I could look extra good for him.

"Oh yeah, it's right . . ."

I dumped two books into his hands so I could open my folder.

"Here. Just give it back to me in chemistry."

After trading books for homework, he gave me a big hug, crushing all the items into my chest.

"That's my girl."

I blushed to the roots of my hair in pleasure. He released me and quickly departed, leaving me standing dumbly in the hall. Pulling myself back together, I looked around the crowded hallway to see if anyone had noticed our exchange.

One person seemed particularly interested, if her narrowed gaze was any indication. Shelby Grant.

I smiled sweetly in her direction and moved toward my first period.

Shelby Grant was a lot of things, and subtle wasn't one of them. So when lunch rolled around and she plopped herself down at the Crew's table, it didn't take a genius to figure out what she was after.

"There you are, Ben." She pouted sweetly, forcing herself between Alyssa and Benjamin, practically dropping herself on his lap in an effort to get close.

"Uh, hey," he said, looking slightly confused. Did he even know her name?

Ignoring his bemusement, she continued undeterred, "I was saying to myself, 'Shelby, where is that Benjamin Hopkins? I bet he could use a copy of last week's notes, since we have a quiz on Wednesday,' and wham, here you are."

Her perfect smile grew in wattage as she produced a copy of the aforementioned notes, and the first thought that crossed my mind was *Whose notes did she copy?* because Shelby wasn't exactly the scholarly type.

"Thanks, Shelby." Ben took the notes she offered, and Alyssa snickered at his use of her name. So convenient of her to use it in the conversation so he would remember her. Hah!

Ignoring Alyssa, Shelby put a hand on Ben's arm and started to yammer away about soccer, of all things, and how she remembered him from when the Beavers played the River View Panthers.

As disconcerting as it was to have the most popular bitch in high school hanging out at our lunch table, it wasn't giving me the epileptic fit that Morgan was experiencing. Justin pretended Shelby wasn't there (smart man) and chatted with Ryan about the usual. Morgan glared daggers at Shelby, and I wondered for a moment if steam was going to erupt from her ears. An intervention was necessary.

"So, Morgan, what did you get on the history test last period?"

She turned toward me and shook her head as though to clear it. "What?"

"You know, Mr. Atkins's quiz on Friday? We got our scores back today. What did you get?"

That seemed to jar her into the here and now, successfully breaking her Shelby train of thought (which I suspect included some form of premeditated homicide), and we tried to act like having Shelby drop into our midst wasn't the most awkward phenomenon in the last millennia.

Alyssa had her own rules about what was fair in love and war. She squirmed around in her seat a moment and

mumbled something about using the bathroom, then jumped away from the table. Shelby smirked in satisfaction as she scooted to take over Alyssa's old seat, then suddenly screeched. We all turned to watch her stand up and survey the rapidly spreading chocolate pudding stain across the ass of her beige suede miniskirt.

I bit my lip to keep from smiling as I turned to watch Alyssa strut across the lunchroom, an empty pudding cup in her hand. She made a big show of dropping it into the garbage can before disappearing into the restroom. Morgan didn't bother hiding the Cheshire cat grin on her face.

Shelby looked around the table in outrage, so I offered her a single square of cafeteria napkin. It was thin enough to see through and not at all effective in removing a cup of pudding from a designer skirt, but it was the most help I was willing to offer.

She grabbed the napkin and immediately fled toward the gym, where the girls' locker room awaited her. She probably had a change of clothes in there. I was relieved she didn't make a mad dash for the restroom in some sort of pudding showdown with Alyssa.

Benjamin looked down at the bench where Shelby had been sitting, and I watched his eyebrows shoot up. Glancing over, I noticed the smudge of pudding, but that certainly wasn't the cause of Benjamin's surprise. Lying open on the bench was Alyssa's purse, with a pregnancy test brazenly exposed.

WTF?

I grabbed her purse, avoiding Benjamin's gaze, and placed it on my other side, next to Morgan. She was surprised by my sudden snatch-and-grab. She caught a glimpse of the pregnancy test.

"That bitch!" she hissed at me.

Though I certainly didn't agree with Alyssa planting a pregnancy test in her purse to fabricate an unexpected and completely fake sexual dilemma, I wasn't sure "bitch" was the right term.

"I can't believe that snake would sink so low," Morgan whispered in my ear. "To put a pregnancy test in Alyssa's bag to sabotage her chances with Benjamin? Of course, it's the only way she could get a man. If she can't steal one out of a relationship, she's going to take out the competition so the playing field is clear. Oh, she's going down. Big-time."

My mouth opened. Did Shelby really plant the test in Alyssa's purse, or had Alyssa put it there hoping it made her appear more sexual? I wish I could share Morgan's outrage, but I wasn't convinced this was all Shelby's doing. When Alyssa wanted something, she plotted all sorts of crazy schemes to

get it. She wouldn't do something hurtful like put a pregnancy test in someone else's purse, but she would totally put one in her own, to give the illusion of experience.

The lunch bell rang, and I stood up on shaky legs. I'd promised to be Switzerland, but I couldn't let Shelby take the fall for this. I caught sight of her marching out of the gym doors, skirt replaced with long shorts, and heard her in my head, clear as day: *You can stop jiggling now.*

I pursed my lips. Okay, maybe I could let her take the fall. It's not like she didn't deserve some sort of slapdown for the countless things she'd done. Sleeping with Justin and making sure Morgan found out about it topped the list and was probably why Morgan was practically foaming at the mouth for revenge. Hell, I could add several humiliating stories where Shelby had me hiding inside the kitchen pantry, inhaling comfort food to feel better. Was it right to punish her for a crime I was almost convinced she didn't commit?

You can stop jiggling now.

Maybe I wasn't rational enough to make that call, so I took up the Switzerland flag again. I'd let karma do its thing. Shelby had jettisoned a lot of bad energy into the universe, and maybe being brought down a peg or two for something she didn't do was karma's way of leveling the field. Who was I to judge the divine nature of things? I stamped down the feelings of guilt and picked up Alyssa's purse to give it back to her.

"Davis, Spencer Davis," Benjamin said as we stood up. "Walk with me and explain what just happened."

He flashed a boyish grin as he gathered up his tray and tossed my empty lunch bag in the garbage.

I threw up my hands in mock confusion, and he laughed. The boy oozed charm. I caught a glimpse of Zachary from the corner of my eye and saw him scowl in my direction. What had he seen? Did he know about the pregnancy test? Hardly. He was too far away to know about that. The pudding sabotage? Surely he would be laughing if that was the case. Was he annoyed that I made Benjamin laugh? That seemed ridiculous, since Zach had spent the lunch hour sitting with the Kessler twins.

What happened to Sydney Porter? Was he done with athletes and wanted to date cowgirls now? Kessler Angus had a cattle ranch on the outskirts of town. The twins had gone to Europe last year with a handful of other students on a cultural road trip that cost bank and included partying in something like five countries, proving that Angus beef must be pretty lucrative.

Zach didn't seem to like Benjamin, and the feeling was mutual as far as I could tell, but to be annoyed at me because I liked Ben was silly. I thought his poem in my locker meant

Serena Robar

he wasn't going to act like this anymore. I tried not to let his scowl affect my mood; however, the walk to class, side by side with Benjamin, lost some of its magic. I wanted to concentrate solely on what Ben was saying. Instead I was craning my neck to see if Zachary was walking with Sydney or one of the Kessler twins.

Did he fill their lockers with sugary sweets this morning?

"Spencer?"

"Huh? What?"

Ben glanced behind us to see what I was looking at. "Are you looking for someone?"

I clutched Alyssa's purse tighter and held it up.

"Yeah, Alyssa left her purse."

"So, that's Alyssa's purse, hmm?"

The expression on his face confirmed that he'd seen the pregnancy test. Great, just great.

Crap.

Alyssa snuck up behind us. "Hey, you grabbed my purse. Thanks for that."

She beamed a high-wattage smile in Ben's direction.

"No problem," I mumbled, completely aware that she wasn't paying me any attention.

"Davis!" Justin called to me from across the busy hallway. I looked at him. He waved me over.

"See ya," I muttered, but they were both in deep conversation about other things and didn't even see me leave.

"What's up?"

Justin opened his locker, so I took a step back to make sure I wasn't crushed by an onslaught of school paraphernalia. He grabbed a drawing and showed it to me. The name "Morgan" was written in urban lettering with some very cool shading. I always thought Justin should take art, but he didn't have any interest in art itself, just doodling letters.

"Very nice."

"It's Morgan's birthday in two weeks, and I'm thinking a great gift would be to tattoo this here." He slapped the paper over his right shoulder blade to get my opinion.

"You want to *tattoo* Morgan's name on your body?"

"Yeah, show her the depth of my emotion, ya know?"

"But you guys break up every other month."

He shrugged. "But we always get back together."

I rubbed my hands over my lids, belatedly realizing I was wearing mascara.

"Shit," I muttered as I tried to wipe and remove any smudging that might have occurred.

"So you don't think it's a good idea?"

I worded my response carefully. If I came across too harsh, he would do it anyway, just to show me he was his own man. If

I simply shrugged, he would take it as an affirmation that his birthday present was brilliant.

"I think the lettering is gorgeous. You know how much I love your artwork, but if you could get someone to take this design and turn it into a necklace, I think Morgan would completely flip for it. *And* she would be able to admire your gift all the time, not just when you two were together."

I held my breath as he thought about what I'd said.

"Fuckin' brilliant, Davis!" He held up his fist to knuckle bump, and I complied. "You have the best ideas. You never let me down."

I smiled weakly, grateful he wasn't going to get the tattoo. Even if it said Morgan. I wasn't anti-tattoo. It's just I was hopelessly practical. What if he broke up with her? What then? How would the next girlfriend feel about another girl's name tattooed on her boyfriend's shoulder? Considering the jealous type of girls Justin went for, I was thinking they would scratch it off his body the first chance they got.

Justin left for class, and I headed in the direction of the library for my study hall. Zach caught up to me just before I reached the door.

"Hey."

"Hey," I returned, keeping my tone as neutral as possible.

"Did you like the poem and the chocolate?" He was

smiling so sweetly that the dimple in his left cheek flashed. My annoyance diminished.

"I did, and thanks for not writing a limerick that required creative rhyming. Very considerate."

He laughed at the reference to his previous masterpiece. "Hey, clitoris and vigorous *do* rhyme, you know."

"Ha! They really don't."

He held open the library door for me. Zach was always doing those kinds of things. Very chivalrous. His mother insisted that he have excellent manners. She said it was the mark of a gentleman.

"Where's the harem?" I asked once we were seated.

"Huh?"

"You know. Sydney Porter, the Kessler twins, yada, yada. You're certainly taking Alyssa's advice to heart about getting out of Ryan's shadow."

"You think I'm dating all those girls?"

"Aren't you?"

He blinked, then let out a bark of laughter that earned him a shush from the librarian. "Thank you."

"Thank you for what?" I hissed in annoyance.

"Thank you for thinking I could date even one of those girls, not to mention all three at the same time."

His grin was contagious. Okay, when he put it that way, it *did* sound kind of ridiculous.

"Then why are you always having lunch with one of them?"

"I'm tutoring them to take the advanced placement math class next year. They have to pass an initial exam to be considered."

"Oh." My face was burning up. This was embarrassing.

"But it's nice to know you care." He bumped my shoulder with his. "Speaking of which, are we on for our usual friendly Winter Formal date night? What color should my tie be?"

I hedged a bit. "Can we talk about it a little closer to the actual dance?"

"Sure. The guys are going in on a limo this year, so it should be fun." I forced a smile.

I wanted Ben to ask me to the dance so I could have a real date. I also didn't want to hurt Zach's feelings. I was being chicken shit, but it would be better to wait and see instead of confessing my hopes and jeopardizing going with Zach.

chapter 14

"Are you ready for Thanksgiving?" I asked Ben in chemistry on Wednesday.

"All the turkey I can eat? Hell, yeah."

Shannon had returned to class, but Mr. Campbell reassigned her to another table. She gave me sour looks the first day, probably because her new partner made her do the experiments.

"What are you doing this weekend?" Ben turned the fire down under the beaker.

"Uh, not sure. Probably Ryan's on Sunday."

"How about you shake things up and go out with me?"

His question didn't register right away, as I was concentrating on measuring our lab assignment, so I blurted, "You want to go out with me?"

"That is, if you want to."

"Of course I want to," I said in a rush.

His answering smile was pure male. "Good, then it's a date."

I pushed the safety glasses back up my sweaty nose and parroted, "It's a date."

"Hey, do you think you can handle the rest of the lab work by yourself? I need to talk with my man Ryan."

Before I could agree, he shot out of his chair and moved to Ryan's workstation. I watched the two Golden Boys tease and plot together. They really did get along great. I wished all my male friends liked Ben as much.

Chewing on my lip, I went back to the experiment. How was I going to tell Alyssa that Ben asked me out? And worse yet, that I accepted? She had no idea that I'd been harboring a crush on Ben since he arrived. It seemed ludicrous to mention out loud, because what would a guy like Ben see in a frump like me? Only he must have seen *something* he liked, because he asked me out. *He asked me out.* I kept the excitement from bubbling up to the surface. I was afraid I would break out into a happy dance in the middle of chemistry class.

Suddenly the air around us turned mustard yellow and the stench was unbearable. Everyone was gagging and plugging their nose, trying to breathe through their mouth. Several students rushed to the windows, pushing to open them. Mr. Campbell covered his nose with a tissue.

"Class, class. Everybody out of the room. Immediate evacuation. Follow the safety procedures. I'm sure we've memorized them by now." He lowered the tissue to clap his hands together. His eyes started to water immediately. He sought out Ryan's station and saw that yellow gas was emanating from their beaker.

"Mr. Payne and uh, Mr. Hopkins, follow me to the principal's office. We'll pick up your mom on the way, Mr. Payne."

All the students poured into the hallway, each one coughing and sputtering. As bad as the odor was, I was more worried about what would happen to Ryan and Ben. Would they get suspended? If so, did that mean Ben would get grounded and our date would be over before it started?

We waited in the hallway as maintenance entered the toxic room and opened the rest of the windows. They let us quickly gather our stuff as soon as some of the gas had dissipated. They locked up the lab for the rest of the day.

Next hour was art, and Ben still wasn't in class. Alyssa

chatted about everything. I kept silent. I didn't know how to tell her that Ben had asked me out. I was such a coward.

I didn't see Ryan or Ben the rest of the day.

I met Alyssa at her car after school. "You're acting weird," she pointed out when I didn't respond to one of her questions. Again.

"Sorry, just worried Ryan is going to get suspended over his latest stunt."

She shook her head. "He can be such an idiot sometimes. And I heard he got Ben in trouble too."

I should have told her right then. I should have confessed that Ben had asked me out in chemistry class, but I didn't. Instead I became the proverbial church mouse as she drove me home. Quiet. Very quiet.

"So it's a safe bet that Sunday is a no-go," Alyssa mused aloud.

"Sunday?"

She gave me another sidelong look. "Yeah, Sunday. Ryan's going to be grounded, at the very least for stinking up the lab."

"Oh, I didn't think of that." My shoulders slumped. That meant Ben's parents would probably ground him as well. Which meant no date this week. Not even a chance encounter on Ryan's stairwell.

"Seriously, what is wrong with you?" Alyssa demanded as we arrived at my house.

My grandmother was in our yard, wearing her housecoat, my black boots with white skulls on them, and what appeared to be a plastic grocery store bag arranged over her hair like a rain cap.

Grandma had had a stroke two years ago and wasn't quite the same in the head. The stroke damaged the part of the lobe that was responsible for personality traits and reasoning. Grandpa usually did a pretty good job watching over her, but disrupting her schedule really messed things up. They were visiting for a week, which was a huge change in her routine, so she was acting more freaky than normal.

Alyssa noticed her at the same time I did and answered her own question. "Never mind, I get it. You gonna be okay?"

Of course, Grandma's eccentricities weren't the reason for my general distracted state, but I wasn't above using her for subterfuge.

I got out of the car but kept the door open and leaned in to confess. "Listen, I have something to tell you."

"Oh, sounds ominous. Did you get a B or something?" she joked.

I took a deep breath. "Ben asked me out."

She looked at me blankly. "Excuse me?"

"I said, Ben asked me out—and, uh, well, I said yes."

"You said yes?"

I nodded.

"But you don't even like Ben!"

"That's not true. I do like him."

"Since when?"

"Since always, actually."

"Yeah, sure you have. Every time I've talked about him and how I was going to make him my first, you'd chime in with how much you wanted him to ask you out."

I flinched at the venom in her voice. "It's not like that."

Her eyes widened. "Really? It's not? 'Cause it feels a lot like my best friend just fucked me over for a guy."

She shoved her car into gear, and I jumped out of the way in time to dodge the open door. I yelled at her to stop, but she wouldn't. The passenger door slammed shut when she stomped on the gas. She was gone.

It wasn't like that, I wanted to scream. *You've got to believe me.*

"Come here, Spencer." My grandmother seemed non-plussed by the exchange.

"Grandma?" I approached her slowly, wondering what to do about Alyssa, when I noticed a large saltshaker in her hand.

"Slugs are Satan's little garden gnomes," she said in disgust.

She shook a dash of salt on a large slug sitting on top of a plant stem, happily munching the last bits of its late-blooming flower. The slug immediately started to dissolve into a white, gooey mess.

Just then the screen door flew open, and my mom, wide-eyed and looking very much harassed, screeched from inside the house, "Mother! What are you doing outside without a coat on? Spencer? What are you doing letting her stand out here in the wet and cold?"

I didn't bother to explain that I'd just arrived and instead ushered Grandma back toward the door. She thrust the shaker into my hand and joined my mother inside.

I looked back at the salted slug. It had fallen from the stem and was writhing on the ground. I kind of felt sorry for it. So it liked the flowers, big deal. Was it wrong to eat the flowers? Should it be persecuted because it wanted something others desired for themselves?

I thought of Benjamin. If I started dating him, it might cost me Alyssa's friendship—a gut-wrenching prospect. Probably not on par with how a slug felt when salted, but certainly painful.

I blew out a frustrated breath. Alyssa would be gone

until Wednesday of the following week, visiting relatives over Thanksgiving. I had to decide what to do about Ben and Alyssa. It wasn't as though I was stealing her boyfriend. They weren't even dating. Somehow I didn't think I could use that argument with her and come out on top, though. The problem was I didn't want to have to choose between Alyssa and Ben. I wanted them both. Was that possible?

The next day the rest of the relatives descended on us en masse. Having the house full, with Grandma behaving so oddly after the stroke, made things really tough on my mom. I thought Grandma was more fun this way, but it must be very disconcerting to her daughters.

"Tell me, Spencer. Did you get my card for your birth-day?" Grandma asked when we'd all sat down to Thanksgiving dinner.

"I did, Grandma. I thanked you when I got it in the mail." She didn't remember things too well either.

"That's right. I forgot. You turned sixteen, right? Did your heathen of a mother take you in to get the Pill?"

Yeah, fun.

"Mother!"

"What? Is it some big secret, Gloria? You've always been out-spoken about your views on sexuality. Don't get prudish now."

I looked at Grandpa, who was smiling and nodding to everyone at the table. I suspected he had his hearing aid turned off. Smart man.

Normally Dad shied away from this kind of talk at the dinner table. When Mom started chatting up birth control or STDs, he would quickly pick up his dinner plate and retire to the living room, turning up the TV so he couldn't hear us anymore. Today was different. Today it was Grandma making Mom uncomfortable, and the small smile on his face suggested that he was enjoying himself.

"Does that mean you're a slut now?" my twelve-year-old cousin asked.

"No, but I *can* be a prostitute. At least they get paid. Sluts just give it away for free."

"Spencer!" My mom was horrified, but everyone else at the table got a good laugh out of it.

The phone rang, and I jumped up to answer it.

"Hello?"

"Happy Thanksgiving!"

"Happy Thanksgiving, Aunt Laverne."

I made a face at the receiver and called for my mom. After she got off the phone with Aunt Laverne, she said, "That's the third time the phone has rung, and each time you jump out of your skin and rush to answer it. Are you expecting a call?"

"Kinda."

I wanted Ben to call and tell me when our date would be. The waiting was driving me insane.

After dinner, the girls gathered all the dishes and congregated in the kitchen to clean up, while the boys went off to watch sports on TV—a time-honored tradition in our house.

I stood next to Grandma, drying dishes. "So, Spencer, are you still a virgin?" she asked me.

"Mother!"

"Shush, I'm talking to Spencer."

"Pure as the driven snow, Grandma." I wasn't surprised by her line of questioning. She'd done the same thing to Heidi when she'd turned sixteen and gotten the Pill.

"Hmph."

I decided to turn the tables and get some old-school advice.

"Were you a virgin when you married Grandpa?"

"Spencer!"

"Shush, the girl's talking to me, Gloria. She knows she can ask me anything."

Mom's lips compressed into a tight line. She attacked the pot in her hand with a scouring brush but remained silent. My aunt and sister tried to hide their grins.

"Yes, Spencer. I was a virgin when I married your grandpa, but it was very close. He could be mighty convincing in his day, if you know what I mean. 'Course there wasn't birth control then, and the man didn't buy the cow if he got the milk for free. Seems like nowadays a man's gotta sample a lot of milk before he commits to a single cow."

Heidi giggled.

Grandma leaned toward me and whispered, "Of course, there are those more free with the samples than others."

I choked on my own laughter, holding the dish towel to my mouth to keep from snorting aloud. Grandma had my sister pegged.

"Do you have a special fellow in mind for the big event, or are you a throwback to my era and going to wait until you're married?"

I noticed that my mother's hands stilled as she waited for my answer.

"I like a guy, but I can't see myself doing anything without love. Real love, not just hormonal love, ya know?"

"My dear Spencer, you have a sound head on your shoulders. You must get that from my side of the family. Grandpa's side is filled with horny little buggers who think with their wangers. Your grandpa is excluded from that category, of course."

Mom was practically having an epileptic fit at the sink, but she was keeping silent. Impressive.

I leaned over and kissed Grandma's leathery cheek. "You're, like, the coolest grandma ever. I love you."

She patted my arm. "Right back at ya. It's easy now, I'm not raising you. I was a different person when your mom was growing up."

Mom snorted in confirmation.

"You turned out all right," Grandma shot back.

"Your influence made Mom the independent, thinking woman she is today, Grandma." Heidi put her arm around Mom to be supportive.

"Suck-up," Grandma whispered to me. I bit down on the drying towel again.

We moved the conversation onto safer topics, where Mom could actually contribute without Grandma shushing her every three seconds. After pie, my grandmother lay down to take a nap. She tired easily these days. God, I loved her. She was such a kick in the pants. I remembered her being much more reserved before the stroke. Now she said whatever she wanted, whenever she wanted. I was totally going to be that way when I was old.

It was Saturday when I got the e-mail from Ben. I was begging Alyssa for forgiveness in one e-mail and finding another one from the object of our affection sitting in my in-box.

Davis—

How about Sunday? I can't leave the house but can
have a study partner come over. Can you be here around three?

Ben

I was excited to get his invite, but a little dubious about
the studying pretext. After all, I seemed to be doing a lot of his
work. I didn't want him assuming I would continue doing his
homework, but I really wanted to see him. I discovered that
when desire and self-respect met, one of them had to take the
backseat. So I made plans to see Ben. I'd let self-respect win
the next round.

Serena Robar

chapter

15

"So, I kind of screwed the pooch for our first date, didn't I?" Benjamin said as he opened the door to greet me. It was Sunday afternoon, and my dad had dropped me off at Ben's house for our "study date," which was the only kind of date his parents would allow because of the chemistry lab incident.

"You are a rock star for coming over to help me."

I blushed in pleasure, especially since his hand brushed my skin when he helped me take off my coat. Mr. Campbell had assigned Ben and Ryan detention and a special assignment as penance for disrupting class. They had to come up with ten safe, nonthreatening formulas that could be used in chemistry lab and write a brief explanation of how to conduct each experiment.

"Ben? Is someone here?" An elegant-looking woman with perfect skin (face-lift?) and a spectacular body (boob job?) stepped out and introduced herself.

"Hello," she said. She gave me her hand, and I shook it. "My name is Shari. I'm Ben's mom, and you must be Spencer. I can't tell you how glad I am that Ben's found a chemistry tutor. Especially now." She rumpled his hair as only a mom could, and Ben stood still, allowing it. He grinned sheepishly in my direction.

I was his tutor?

"So, Davis, I have everything set up for us downstairs." He grabbed my bag, and I was relieved to follow.

"It's nice to meet you," I told his mother, who beamed a teeth-whitened smile back at me.

Ben led me through the living room and down a flight of stairs to the basement. It was obviously his hangout, because it had all sorts of guy sports stuff and posters on the wall. The lighting was dim, and Ben took me over to a well-worn couch. He dropped my bag on the scuffed coffee table and offered me a soda. It was nothing like Ryan's basement, but it seemed like this was where Ben *lived*, and the intimacy of that made me hyperaware of his presence.

"Sorry about the whole tutor thing. Trust me, it was the only *way* I was going to be able to see you this weekend."

"No big." I didn't want him to know that I was disappointed he didn't introduce me to his mom as just a girl he wanted to see. "We could have waited until you were off grounded."

I sat down, and he plopped down beside me.

"But I didn't want to wait." He gave me a slow, sexy smile, and I was grateful to be sitting down, since my stomach fluttered nervously.

He leaned forward and opened my bag, taking out the chemistry book and binder. I gave him a questioning look.

"Subterfuge. Mom will be down in a sec to check up on us."

Sure enough, Shari reappeared on the squeaky stairs, popping her perfectly styled head around the corner.

"You kids want some snacks?"

I soon had my laptop out and was connected to his wireless Internet, searching for experiments that fit Mr. Campbell's requisites, while Ben wrote them down and copied the correlating elemental formula chart. Though Ben assured me he would do the assignment on his own later tonight, it was a simple matter to search for formulas online and give him a head start. He protested at first, but we were already on the fourth one when his mom came back with the snacks, soda and some chips. I noticed her looking over Ben's shoulder, checking out what we'd accomplished so far. We must have passed muster, because she gave me another bright smile and left us alone.

"We should be good for a while now."

I wasn't sure what to do now that we were alone on our "date" and weren't going to be interrupted. Nervous, I went back to reciting the next formula and condensing the instructions for Ben to copy. In no time we were on the eighth problem, and Ben announced that it was break time.

He took my computer off my lap and set it gently down on the table, next to the book and his notes. I nervously reached for a chip, but when it was halfway to my mouth I paused. I didn't want food in my mouth if he was going to kiss me, did I?

I couldn't really put the chip back now that it was in my hand, and I didn't want to chew it up. I wanted him to try to kiss me. Ugh! What was I going to do?

Ben solved my problem by plucking the chip out of my hand and eating it. I let out my breath, unaware that I'd been holding it.

"So, where's your dad today?" I asked.

"Golfing," Ben replied, his mouth still crunching on the chip.

"Do you golf?"

"Nah, I prefer soccer."

Ben was wearing a loose soccer jersey and long shorts. His

legs were strong and surprisingly tan. I figured he would have paled out more, but his skin was golden and flecked with soft brown hair. He looked comfortable. I would have been freezing, especially since his basement was notably cooler than the upstairs. Why did guys always wear shorts into the winter?

I shivered.

"Are you cold?" He pulled a small blanket off the back of the couch.

"No, I—" His arms reached around me to position the blanket over my shoulders, and the gesture silenced me. We were face-to-face, and he was holding me in place by the ends of the blanket. I looked into his very green eyes and saw him gaze down at my lips. Was this it? Would he kiss me?

Instead of leaning toward me, he gently pulled the blanket closer to him, effectively coaxing my entire body closer to his. My hair was loose and efficiently pinned down under the blanket so it wasn't in my face. I watched his mouth move closer to mine.

This was it. He was going to kiss me again.

Suddenly his lips were on mine, and I closed my eyes. They were soft, warm, and salty from the chips. I felt his lips move, so I gently opened mine, praying I was doing the right thing. I'd never given anyone an openmouthed kiss before, and I didn't want to be the girl who produced too much spit or opened her mouth too wide or licked like a dog. I was so afraid of doing it wrong, so I chose inaction. I waited for him to take the lead.

And boy, did he lead. I'd suspected Ben had been around the block when it came to women, but I wasn't prepared for how skilled his kisses were. His moist tongue (not too much saliva, totally perfect) swept into my mouth and sort of coaxed mine to swirl around his. I was nervous. Did he think I was an amateur? Was I doing it right?

His mouth gently pulled away from mine. He pressed his lips against my jawline, moving toward my ear. Soft butterfly kisses that might have been tickling if I wasn't so crazed from all the sensations that were assaulting me.

"Relax," he whispered gently in my ear, and I tried to let go of the tension in my shoulders. He released the blanket and nudged me, never breaking the connection his lips had on my skin. One arm pulled me closer, while the other braced the back of the couch, balancing us, as he shifted his weight over my body.

Was I cold before? I couldn't remember ever being cold. My skin was hot, and my whole body trembled. Ben's lips returned to mine, getting more aggressive.

His kisses were making me squirm. I grabbed at his shoulders and back, trying to get even closer. His body was resting fully on mine, his hips cradled between my legs. I felt so small under his weight. One hand dug into my hair and the other dropped to my waist. He pulled at the belt loop of my jeans, urging me closer to him.

I couldn't think clearly. I was breathless and overflowing with sensations. What if his mother came down to check on us? Ben's hand slipped under my shirt effortlessly, and I practically bucked us off the coach when his hand cupped my breast.

"Whoa!" I gasped, pulling away.

"Shhh," he responded, stilling his hand and brushing his lips against mine. "Shhh, just let me touch you."

His voice was soft and soothing. It calmed me, and his kisses were so good, I didn't want to stop. I just wasn't sure I was ready for even more.

"Ben?" His mouth silenced the rest of my words. What was I going to say? I couldn't really remember, and thinking was becoming more and more difficult. He repositioned his body, his hips sliding across mine, and I gasped. Wow. His body next to mine was amazing.

The hand near my breast moved again, slowly. Not only was my body trembling, now my extremities were visibly shaking. If I was forced to play a game of Operation right now, I would never be able to pull out any of the pieces without setting off the buzzer, my hands shook that bad. He rubbed my breast over my bra, causing the nipple to harden. I felt a tugging sensation between my legs. I wanted him to touch more skin. His lips were on my neck, and I wanted them to go lower. This was not supposed to be happening. Not now, in the basement of Ben's house, with his mom upstairs, ready to drop in on us with a fresh bag of chips without notice.

"Ben, please." What I was pleading for was up for debate at this point. Was I begging him to stop or to continue? My body knew what it wanted, but my mind was confusing the issue with reason and logic.

"Your mom might . . ." His hand stopped and reluctantly inched away from my breast. He took a steadying breath, propped himself up, and looked down at me. The hand that had once been beneath my shirt now raked through his hair. His eyes had never looked greener. His lips were swollen, and his skin was flushed.

"Spencer, I want you so bad." He punctuated that statement by rubbing his jean-clad erection against my leg.

Holy cow!

"Ben, I—"

"How are you kids doing down there?"

We both froze for about a half a second before jumping up and grabbing our study materials.

"Fi—" Ben's voice cracked, so he cleared his throat and tried again. "Fine."

"It's getting close to dinnertime, Ben, so maybe you should take Spencer home? Only there and back—remember, you're still grounded."

"Okay, Mom," he called out loudly, so she wouldn't feel the need to come down the stairs to tell us again.

I stood up on shaky legs and closed my laptop quickly, not bothering to shut it down. Ben helped gather the other things, and I was pleased to note that his hands shook as well.

"Let's sneak out these doors down here so we don't run into my mom again. Your skin is bright red from my whiskers." He smiled at me, and I smiled back.

He grabbed some keys and called out to his mom that we were leaving, then hurried out the door before she could protest.

Once we were seated in his car and I told him what direction to go, I remembered. "We didn't get all the questions done."

He grinned in my direction. "I think the break was worth it."

I laughed. I thought things would be weird, but they weren't so different. We still teased each other and laughed. Maybe having sex with someone didn't have to change everything. Sure, we'd only fooled around a little, but it wasn't making me crazy or obsessed.

"You know, I get off grounded in two weeks."

Please ask me out again. Please ask me out again.

"Uh-huh," I said instead, trying to play it cool.

"And I hear there's something called a Winter Formal coming up."

"I've heard of it."

"So maybe you and I should go?"

"Maybe we should."

"Then it's a date." He grinned at me.

"It's a date."

We arrived at my house in record time. He kissed me quickly, citing his need to get home so he didn't get in more trouble, and I slipped out of the car.

I watched him drive away and walked toward the house, still warm from Ben's touch, when I realized I'd left my coat at his house.

Oh, well. With Ben around I would never be cold again.

On Monday morning I paid extra-close attention to my appearance. Were Ben and I a couple now? Was it naive to think we would hold hands in the hallway and sneak kisses between classes, because of what happened in his basement? I didn't know. I was so new to all this. He asked me to Winter Formal, but that didn't mean we were a couple. I would know what to do when I saw him at school. I would let him set the tone.

I was giving him all the power in our burgeoning relationship, which was a bad idea. I'd seen enough *Oprah* to figure that out, but I didn't know how to take that power back. I'd never had a boyfriend, and he was more experienced than I was. It was better to just wait and see. At least I hoped so.

When I saw Benjamin in the hallway, our eyes locked and he gave me a devilish wink. Just between him and me. I blushed and smiled back. He didn't approach me, so I went to first period feeling a bit disappointed.

After class ended, Zach met me by our lockers. I was loading up my backpack when Shelby Grant, followed by her minion wannabes (Kristi and Marissa), moved in behind me.

"Congratulations, Spencer," Shelby said, sounding almost sincere. "Getting Ben to ask you to Winter Formal. What's your little buddy going to do?" She gave Zach a meaningful look, and they left me. How did she know?

"Ben asked you to Winter Formal?" Zach demanded. "And you said yes?"

"I—"

"What about our plans, Spencer?"

"If you'll just let me explain," I stammered.

He stood in silence, waiting.

Except I really couldn't explain, could I? Ben asked me and I said yes, even though I knew Zach assumed we were going together. There wasn't much to explain after all.

He threw up his hands, muttering, "Whatever," and walked away.

Shelby, smelling blood, returned to me and said, "Wow, he still thought you two were going together. That was really cold, Davis. Who knew you could be such a bitch?"

I felt the tears start to fall as I turned away and fled down the hall, her taunting laughter following me.

Morgan found me hiding out in the back stall.

"You've been a busy girl."

"I take it you talked to Zach?"

"Nope, Alyssa called me Sunday."

I groaned, wrinkling my nose at the stale cigarette smell in the bathroom.

"You still have Zach," she said, trying to cheer me up.

"I don't think Zach wants to talk to me right now."

"Don't tell me he's mad at you too?"

I shrugged. "He mentioned going to the dance together last week, and I told him we'd talk about it later. Then Ben asked me and I said yes."

"So it's a safe bet that Zach's feelings are hurt."

"You know, we came up with the 'going as friends' to the

  Serena Robar

dance years ago because neither of us had a real date. It's just sort of evolved to every major dance. When he brought it up this time, he made it sound like it was a done deal. I just didn't know what to say. Ben hadn't asked me yet, so I didn't say anything, because if he didn't I still wanted to go to the dance with Zach."

Morgan cringed when I said it out loud. It sounded bad. Really bad.

"I'm a royal bitch, aren't I?"

"Maybe just on paper."

I knew the truth when I heard it. "I was using Zach as a safety net. I was totally using him. Omigod. I really *am* a royal bitch."

She patted my shoulder in sympathy.

"Liking a boy can get you into all kinds of shit, can't it?"

"Morgan, I've always liked Ben. Since the first day I saw him in the parking lot, I've liked him."

"Why didn't you say something then?"

"Why should I? It's not like I thought I had a shot."

"And you think Alyssa had a better shot than you?" Her voice was incredulous.

I stared at her dumbly. "Of course."

"So if he'd asked Alyssa, you would have smiled and congratulated her, but inside you'd be a crying mess."

I shuffled my feet. "I'm not sure 'crying' is the right word."

"Fine. You'd be a mess."

"Maybe. But I swear I'd have been happy for her. I wouldn't blame her or anything."

"And you think that's how Alyssa should be acting right now?"

"God, no. She should be pissed off. I broke the friendship code. I never should have agreed to go out with Ben."

She nodded and blew out a breath. "Tell me, Spencer. Why is it okay for Alyssa to get pissed at you over a guy, but it's not okay for you to do it?"

"Huh?"

"I don't think Alyssa is the type of girl who expects her friends to sacrifice their own happiness because you both want the same thing. She's a better friend than that."

"Of course she is! I'm the crappy friend in this scenario."

"But what about your happiness? Don't you think she'd want you to be happy too? Her liking Ben wasn't about Ben at all. It was about her 'getting laid' goal. You actually like him as a person."

I nodded slowly. I did like Ben.

"Then I think she'll forgive you without your having to give up your own happiness along the way."

"You think it's going to be that easy?"

"Hell, no. I see serious groveling in your future, but eventually she'll come around. Just don't rush her. But you need to tell her about Winter Formal before she gets back to school and hears it from someone else."

I hugged Morgan. "You're a good friend. Now what do I do about Zach?"

She shook her head in exasperation. "Dude, that's all I got. Figure Zach out on your own."

She left me standing in the stall, thinking about what she'd said. I needed to grovel but give Alyssa some space and time to cool off. The wonders of text messaging and e-mails should put me on the right road; now what about Zach? That was going to require a face-to-face, and sooner rather than later. Zach tended to stew and make himself even more upset the longer something went on. But would he let me get close enough to make it right? That was the question.

He avoided me at school, and my e-mails to Alyssa went unanswered. I told her about Ben asking me to Winter Formal. I confessed all the feelings I was having inside and how much I wished I could talk to her. I was beginning to doubt she would forgive me, but at least she heard about the dance from me.

The next evening Zach still hadn't called. I debated whether or not to call again but discarded the idea. I was not going to be an apology stalker. I would give him one more day, and then

I was going over to his house to have this out. He knew how much I hated waiting or having anyone I cared about mad at me. Not calling me back was the perfect punishment for me.

Wednesday arrived, and Alyssa didn't come to school. I wondered if her vacation was extended or if she was avoiding me. And Ben—well, Ben was charming, but elusive. Once in a while he walked with me to our class and he flirted with me, but then that was in his nature. Nothing to lead me to believe that our time together in his basement meant more to him than a fling. I wanted to bring it up, but I didn't want to risk ruining Winter Formal. I was such a dork. If I were more experienced I would know what to do. I would know how to act. Instead I just played it cool and let Ben lead. Sadly, he was leading us in no certain direction and he seemed fine with that. Men.

I couldn't pin Zach down at school. He just looked through me like I wasn't even there.

I started to get mad. No, pissed actually. He couldn't keep avoiding me. It wasn't healthy. I asked Morgan to drop me off at Zach's house instead of taking me home.

"Are you sure you don't want me to wait, in case you need a ride home?" The unspoken scenario of Zach refusing to see me hung in the air.

"Nope. He can't ignore me if I'm camped on his doorstep."

"You're the boss. Good luck." I watched her drive away.

I approached the front door and knocked. Mrs. Thames was surprised to see me, but delighted all the same. She ushered me inside to the living room and called Zach down.

Zach trudged down the stairs and paused at the bottom when he spotted me.

"Hey," I said.

He didn't say anything.

"Still giving me the silent treatment? Not that I blame you. I was a royal b-i-t-c-h. Undeserving of a friend of your magnitude."

Still he said nothing.

I blew out a breath.

Silence.

"Please, Zach. I hate that I've hurt you. I have an ache in my stomach that won't go away. I can't fall asleep at night because I can't stop thinking about the pain I caused you. I was selfish and wrong and"—I took a shaky breath—"I can't stand the thought of us not being friends. I really can't."

When he didn't say anything, I had to look away. I dropped my head and sniffed, willing the tears not to flow. I didn't want to add guilt to his anger. His anger was justified. If he needed time, then I would give him time.

"I'll just go," I whispered, turning to leave. I took two steps and walked into something warm and solid. Zach had silently moved from the stairs to block my path. His strong arms wrapped around me. I couldn't hold back the tears and sobbed into his shoulder.

"I'm sorry, I'm sorry, I'm sorry," I kept blubbering.

"Shhhh, don't cry."

He held me, crooning softly, and the knot in my stomach slowly eased. A new sensation flooded my stomach. A jittery, fluttery sensation. I started to take note of how solid Zach felt and how strong his arms were. He was stroking my hair, while his other arm held me against him.

I took another shaky breath that had nothing to do with my tears. What was happening to me? I felt electric. My skin was hypersensitive to Zach's touch, and my blood was racing in my veins. This had to be from the emotional release of my breakdown. The only other time I felt remotely like this was when Ben was around. And even then it wasn't this intense.

I pulled away gently and looked up at Zach. He used his finger to wipe away any remaining tears on my cheeks.

"I'm sorry," I hiccuped again.

"I know. I shouldn't have shut you out like that. You never committed to going to the dance with me. It was just that we usually go together. I'm sorry I made you suffer."

"No, I deserved to suffer. I would never hurt you on purpose, you've gotta know that—"

"Shhh. It's okay, Spencer. All is forgiven. I was a dick to wait so long. I don't want to hurt you, either."

"So we're really okay?"

"Yeah." We hugged again to seal the deal. My entire body tingled where it touched his. I told myself the shiver I experienced in his arms was from emotional stress.

We awkwardly pulled out of the embrace. Our cheeks were high with color. Zach coughed and took a step backward. "Do you need a ride home?"

I took another step backward as well. "Uh, yeah, that would be great."

"Let me find my keys."

I watched him move around the room, gathering his shoes and looking for his keys. My heart was beating hard, and I still felt tingly where our bodies had touched. Suddenly I couldn't get out of his house fast enough, and I sensed he felt the same way. We made it to my house in record time.

"Thanks for the ride, Zach." I pushed open the door and practically fell onto the driveway. He backed out, and his tires literally screeched on the pavement when he drove away. I watched him barrel down the road and turn. I pressed my hand to my heart. It was still racing.

chapter

16

By the next day at
school, I'd convinced myself any feelings I experienced over
at Zach's were typical of relief that he'd forgiven me. I wasn't
Shelby Grant. I didn't switch my affections to a new guy
each week. I was mistaken when I thought it was Zach who
caused my blood to pump and my heart to race. It was relief.
Period.

"Hey," I said to Zach in the hallway.

"Hey," he replied, not quite meeting my eyes.

It was going to take a couple of days for the weirdness
between us to go away. That's how it was when such good

friends had a fight. There was that readjustment period. Now if only Alyssa could forgive me.

She was opening her locker when I approached.

"Hey," I said softly.

She took a deep breath and muttered "Hey" in return.

"Did you get my e-mails?"

"Yeah." Short. Concise. To the point.

"And?" I prodded gently.

"And what, Spencer?" She slammed her locker closed and looked at me.

"You can't forgive me, can you? Nothing I can say will make this better between us, will it?"

She took a moment to consider the question, then posed her own. "Would you break it off with Ben if I asked?"

I took a step back in surprise.

"Well, would you?"

"Are you saying I have to choose between my friendship with you and a date with Ben?"

"What if I was?"

"Then I would have to re-evaluate our friendship."

"What?!"

"A friend, a real friend, wouldn't ask me to do that. I didn't steal Ben away from you. He just liked me more and asked me out. I should have told you how I felt about him but I didn't, and for that I'm sorry. But asking me not to see him just so you feel better isn't something a real friend would do."

She looked shocked, and I regretted the loss of our friendship. I loved Alyssa like a sister and would give her anything in my power, but I wouldn't sacrifice myself in the process. Morgan was right. It wasn't that I thought Ben was more important than she was, because I didn't. But what kind of relationship did she and I have if she expected me to give up things that were important to me just because she couldn't have them? I understood that now.

She was slow to respond.

"You were wrong not to tell me how you felt about Ben. I felt betrayed when you told me he asked you out, Spencer. I was jealous, pure and simple, because him falling for you had nothing to do with me liking him. I should have been a better friend and been happy for you. I can forgive you for not telling me you liked Ben if you can forgive me for giving you the silent treatment for so long. And no, I would never ask you to give up someone you cared about to prove your loyalty to me."

"Really?" I was incredulous.

"Yeah, really. You're my best friend, and it was never really about Ben as a person. He was just one of the guys on the list. Sure, he's hot, but there are other cute guys out there."

I threw my arms around her, and we hugged. Zach

surprised us both by sneaking up and joining in the group hug. Then so did Morgan, Justin, and finally Ryan. We were all laughing.

"Who's grabbing my ass?" Morgan demanded when she saw both of Justin's hands in the air.

"Sorry." Ryan laughed, earning him a shove from Justin. They dispersed down the hallway to go to their classes.

"So it looks like you and Zach patched things up," Alyssa said.

"Yeah, everything is great."

"You don't seem like everything is great."

I chewed on my lip. "Are we still going to the dance as a group? I would understand if you didn't want to share the limo."

She waved her hand. "Of course I want us to go together. I can handle it, Spencer. I just have to find a date."

I nodded. "I have no idea what I'm going to wear."

"Gotcha. I already have a dress. I picked it up cheap last year, when all the prom dresses went on sale."

"You are so organized. It really is disgusting."

She shrugged. "It's a gift, baby. See you at lunch."

I hadn't really thought of what I was going to wear until I mentioned it to Alyssa. Now it consumed my mind. I had no idea what to wear. What would Ben be wearing? We had to match, right?

I'd worked myself into a fine state by lunchtime. I couldn't even eat, I was so nervous.

"Are you gonna eat that sandwich, Davis?" Ryan asked, already reaching for it.

I shook my head and pushed it in his direction. Ben perused my food choices and pantomimed being a puppy, whining and nudging me with his nose, pawing at my dessert.

I relented and gave him the Hostess cupcake. Justin just reached over and grabbed the last item, a bag of chips. I noted Zach sitting next to Tiara Kessler (or was it Cheyenne?). I gave him a brief wave, and he nodded.

"Have you ordered your tux yet?" I asked Ben in chemistry.

"Huh?"

"For the dance. Your tux?" I reminded him.

"No, my mom is taking me this weekend. I guess I have to try the jackets on or something. Lame."

"You're going to need to know my dress colors before you order the corsage."

"Corsage?"

"Yeah, the little bunch of flowers I wear during the dance. You get a boutonniere to wear that matches."

"So what color is it? And please don't say mauve or something weird. I need it in guy terms. Like red or yellow." He gave me a charming smile.

"Let's make this easy, shall we? I order them, and you just pick them up the day of the dance."

"Really? You'd do that? Sweet." He high-fived me. I tried not to roll my eyes. We hadn't kissed since that day on his couch. He treated me like he did the other members of the Crew. I didn't want him thinking of me as one of his soccer buddies. I wanted him thinking of me as something much more intimate.

I was wondering if our date was really that—a date. Were we just friends going to Winter Formal together? Was feeling up girls in his basement so commonplace to him that he'd forgotten it was me that night on his couch? Just when I was convinced that must be the case, he would put his arm around me and whisper how much he was looking forward to holding me in his arms and I would be confused all over again.

After the stinky lab incident, Ryan wasn't allowed near the lab equipment unsupervised. Mr. Campbell was his new lab partner. Ryan had to do all the work himself. If his expression was any indication, I sensed he would need to do something chaotic and dramatic soon before the pressure to walk the straight and narrow became too much for him.

Ryan needed upheaval around him on a regular basis. I had

no idea why; it's just the way he was. He'd been banned from shop class after he dared poor Tyler Artson to use the band saw blindfolded. It was a dumb-ass thing for Tyler to do. I'm just glad they found the tip of his finger so they could sew it back on.

The home ec teacher still burst into tears whenever she saw him walking down the hallway. Now that Mr. Campbell had put the kibosh on his chemistry high jinks, it was only a matter of time until the people closest to him suffered. I waited with mixed emotions. When Ryan submitted to his darker side, it would be big. Huge.

It was the beginning of winter break.

"We're never going to decide on a dress if we all go," I remarked, irritated that we were already running twenty minutes late and hadn't even left the house.

"You need me because Sheryl is my friend," said Heidi, pulling her coat on and grabbing her purse.

"You need me because I'm your best friend," Alyssa put in.

We all looked at my mother. "You need me because I have the money."

Trump card.

"I still don't know why you can't just wear a dress in your closet. You have several in there," my dad said.

We looked at Dad in horror. "But I've *worn* those dresses already."

"Daddy, she can't wear those again!"

"Mr. Davis, no one wears the same formal dress twice."

It was a chorus of protests. Finally we all looked to Mom for guidance.

"Dear, there are larger things at work here that you can't possibly understand."

"But I can pay for?" he added drily.

"Don't worry, Dad. The dress is for me, remember? I'm all about the sales." I reached up and kissed him on the cheek, and then everyone piled into the car.

Mom drove us to the mall, where Heidi's friend Sheryl had selected several gowns for me to try on. Sheryl was a personal shopper who'd scoured the mall and had each store set aside possibilities before we got there. It was supposed to make dress shopping easier, but with so many varying opinions in the car, I doubted we would agree on a single garment.

Alyssa bragged about her dress purchase. Her entire ensemble, including shoes and clutch bag, had cost fifty-eight dollars and change. She was amazing.

I wanted to find something that would make me look twenty pounds thinner and four inches taller and would cause heads to turn when I walked into a room. I figured by the end of the day I would be happy to find something that fit slightly better than a burlap sack and didn't cost a year's college tuition.

We arrived at Nordstrom and met Sheryl at the concierge desk.

Sheryl had gone to high school with Heidi. She'd worked at the Brass Plum after school for years, and instead of going the college route, her eye for fashion landed her a personal shopper position. She greeted us, dressed impeccably. I was grateful she was willing to help us out. She wasn't making any money doing this for us, especially since she prescouted clothes at the competition, but she and Heidi were best friends, and there was nothing they wouldn't do for each other.

"I've got our afternoon all mapped out," she addressed us with authority. "First we start here, then Macy's and Penney's, and from there we hit the smaller stores like Mariposa, BCBG, and such. We will totally find the perfect dress for you, Spencer. I bet my reputation on it."

"This is going to be expensive, isn't it?" I chewed on my lower lip in apprehension.

Sheryl winked. "Trust me."

We headed upstairs to a huge dressing room that was practically overflowing with formal wear. She had me try on

all sorts of dresses in all shapes and sizes. She wanted to see everything on me, no matter how hideous.

"How can trying *this* dress on possibly help our search? I would never wear this in public."

The fuchsia beaded gown fit like a second skin in a very unflattering way, with the spaghetti straps digging into my shoulders. The price tag was eight hundred dollars.

Sheryl made a clicking sound with her tongue. "Oh, ye of little faith. What all these dresses are showing me is what components of each compliment you. Do you want to know what I've learned so far?"

Alyssa and Mom were seated in chairs facing the three-way mirror. Heidi was helping me put on and take off dresses. They shouted "Yes!" in unison.

"Spencer is very curvy. Very hourglass. We want something that tucks around her middle, but flows from there down. Maybe even an empire waist. Also, a lower neckline would be flattering, but nothing strapless. She's too top-heavy for that. She can't wear the jewel tones. They wash her out. She needs something more muted to complement her pale skin. If we found something with a three-quarter sleeve, that would be great, but it's not required. She can wear a taller shoe since her date is tall, but I would want it to be a wide heel, so she doesn't teeter and worry about falling over all night."

My mouth was hanging open. "You learned all that from me trying on these dresses?"

"Of course," my sister bragged. "She's the *best*. I told you."

"Now that we know what we're looking for, go change back into your street clothes and we'll head out to those other stores and find a dress that doesn't break the bank."

And just like that we made the rounds. Sheryl flipped through the racks, clicking her tongue and pulling out only the dresses that fit her requirements. I tried to pull out some that I thought would work, but after being shot down several times when she pointed out the "problems" of each of my choices, I wisely shut up and let the professional do her thing.

At the third store I knew I'd found the dress. It was a gorgeous flowing cream number with gold thread weaved through it, gathering at the waist and flowing down the body. Large, citrinelike gems adorned the inch-wide shoulder straps. It reminded me of something a Grecian goddess would wear. I pictured myself walking into the room, the pale material swirling all around me, hair piled high on my head in ringlets, capturing the attention of everyone there.

Once it was on my body, everyone agreed. No more looking. This was it. And it only took us two and a half hours. Next we searched for sandals to match, which was a little trickier, but success was ours after another hour. No jewelry, except gold slave bracelets high on the arms fitted over matching gauze scarves to disguise my chunky upper arms.

In celebration we gorged ourselves on hamburgers, treating Sheryl to lunch for all her help, and left the restaurant with cash to spare.

"It's rarely this easy," Sheryl mused. "I expected this to take all day and then some, but your lucky stars were all lined up or something."

We returned home with our booty. Dad demanded to know the damage, and even he was impressed by the low total.

"Aren't you going to try it on to show me?"

"No way. It needs the hair and makeup and everything just right for the full effect. You'll see it at Winter Formal, Dad."

"You girls usually make me sit through a fashion show."

"You'll see it in a couple of weeks. Until then you'll just have to wait." Mom kissed him to soften the blow as we raced upstairs.

I hung the dress up on my closet door so I could admire it some more.

"I should have brought my dress over so we could see how great we'll look side by side at the dance," Alyssa said.

She cocked her head, critically assessing my gown. "Since my dress is turquoise and strapless, we'll be a great contrast."

"I'll come home that weekend to do your hair, Spence," Heidi generously offered.

I felt moisture gather in my eyes and took a deep breath. I was a bit overwhelmed. Everyone was making this dance so special for me, especially Alyssa. She could have harbored resentment that Benjamin had asked me instead of her, especially after the way she found out. But Alyssa hadn't been petty. Truth be told, she took it much better than I would have, if the situation had been reversed.

"Will you tell me who your mystery date is now, Alyssa?" I whined.

"Nope, not yet."

"I don't know why you're making me wait." I went from whiny to pouty in less than three seconds.

She came back to me and took my hands into hers. She looked me deep in the eye. "My date for Winter Formal . . ."

"Yes?"

"Is staying a mystery until that night."

I blinked. Twice. Heidi burst out laughing.

"You are *such* a turd," I huffed, pulling my hands out of her grasp.

Alyssa smiled mysteriously. "All things shall be revealed in their proper time. You must have patience, grasshopper."

"I hate waiting."

"It's only three weeks, and we're on winter break two of those. I think you'll survive."

"You're really not going to tell me, are you?"

"Nope."

"The gossip mill will tell me. There are no secrets at May Valley."

She gave me a little smile. I had a feeling only she and the guy she was going with knew, and I bet she'd sworn him to secrecy.

The phone rang, and Heidi picked up. She took it out of the room to speak in private.

"At least tell me you've given up the crazy scheme to lose your virginity on dance night."

She looked perplexed. "Why would I?"

"Why would—? 'Cause you're not going with Ben, that's why."

"So? Ben was only one name on the list. Granted, it's a setback. The players may have changed, but the goal stays the same."

I bit my tongue, literally, to keep from screaming in frustration. She was tenacious. Who was on the list? I tried to remember the names. Justin was going with Morgan. I didn't know who Ryan was taking. Maybe he was Alyssa's mystery date.

"Fine. Keep your secrets. I just wish you'd reconsider the one-night-stand approach."

"Instead of thinking about what's going to happen on my date, you might want to focus on what could happen on yours. Ben obviously likes you, or he wouldn't have asked you to the dance. What if he gets a hotel room and wants to take your relationship to the next level? What are you going to do then?"

What would I do then? I really liked Ben, but was I ready to sleep with him? Instead of answering her very real question, I went for the joke.

"Why, I'd send you in my stead, of course."

We laughed, and Alyssa dropped her line of questioning. I didn't know what I was going to do if Ben got a room. I hoped I wasn't going to be faced with that dilemma. I was afraid I didn't know what my answer would be, and that worried me more than anything.

chapter

17

"You look radiant," Mom told me, touching one of the springing ringlets around my face.

"Yeah, and your hair looks great," my sister joked.

"Must be my hairdresser."

"She's the best," Heidi agreed, preening because she, in fact, had styled my hair.

"Will the pearls stay in?" asked Mom.

"Yep, I weaved them through her hair and clipped each section in place. See, here." My sister showed her masterpiece to my mother, lifting a small section of hair to reveal the clip fastener.

"Ingenious. The effect is amazing. You *do* look just like an Olympian goddess."

I beamed in pleasure. I hoped Benjamin would think so too. The only cloud over my night was the weirdness with Zachary. He would be in the limo with his date, and I hated to think it would be strained between us all evening.

"You don't think I'm showing too much boob, do you?" I tried to pull the material up a little, and my sister shooed my hands away.

"Stop that, you'll rip it or something. It's perfect. You're gonna knock his socks off."

Mom coughed nervously and took one of my hands.

"Now, Spencer. Tonight is a big night, and everyone looks so lovely, but don't let the lights and the finery go to your head. Remember to stay sober and make good choices."

"I'm not much of a partier, Mom. You know that's Heidi's domain," I joked. Heidi gasped and leaned forward to smack the back of my head, but stopped at the last minute.

"I'd bop you upside the head for that, but I don't want to ruin all my hard work."

The doorbell rang, and all three of us jumped. It was Ben. It had to be. Both of them gave me the once-over, straightening my shoulder strap or pulling a curl into place, while my father appeared from nowhere to open the front door.

Serena Robar

"Dad," I hissed.

"If the boy is dating my daughter, I want to meet him."

Mom patted my shoulder as if to say Dad wouldn't embarrass me.

The door swung open, and the breath caught in my throat. It was a collective gesture, because my mom and Heidi had the same reaction. Benjamin was stunning in a tuxedo. Even my dad paused a moment.

"Mr. Davis?" Ben asked, putting his hand out to shake. "It's nice to meet you. I'm here to pick up your daughter for our . . ."

Ben's voice trailed off when he looked over my dad's shoulder and saw me standing there. His eyes widened, and his gaze swept over my appearance, settling over my chest longer than my face, but the dress did display cleavage. I smiled in return.

"Davis, Spencer Davis. You look amazing." I blushed in pleasure, and so did my mother.

Dad took Ben's offered hand, which was still hanging in the air, and invited him in.

Ben wore a traditional black tux, but his cummerbund and tie were gold brocade to match my dress. I'd given him one of my arm scarves so he could match the colors. He returned it to me with a flourish. "For you."

I took the offering and tucked it under the bare slave bracelet so it matched the other arm.

"Also for you."

He slipped the cream and gold rose corsage that I'd ordered onto my wrist. My sister introduced herself, as did my mom. She made us pose for endless pictures. Dad stood far off in the corner, looking a bit misty-eyed.

"We'd better go, since we have the limo," Ben said, guiding me to the door. My sister handed me my new gold clutch, and Dad slipped something into Ben's hand on the sly.

When we were outside I asked, "What did my dad give you?"

Ben opened his hand and revealed a fifty-dollar bill.

I gasped in surprise.

"Good thing he did, 'cause after the tux rental and limo, I'm broke. We were gonna have to eat at Mickey D's."

I searched his face to see if he was serious, and he laughed. "Come on, Aphrodite. Your chariot awaits."

The boys had pooled their resources and rented a limo for the night. It was a huge stretch and sat ten comfortably. There were four couples, so we should have plenty of room.

I was surprised again when the limo driver hopped out of the car to open our doors for us.

"Billy Conlin?"

"Hey, Spencer. You look hot."

Billy was in the same class as my sister. His father owned the limo company, and instead of heading off to college, Billy was learning the family business from the ground up.

"What were the odds you'd be our driver tonight?" I asked.

"Pretty good, since I owe Justin a favor and he's cashing in tonight."

I didn't know what the favor was, but the boys must be getting a deal on the transportation.

"Hop in."

Climbing into a limo in a long formal gown was not a graceful experience. I pulled the lightweight material up so my legs wouldn't get entangled and slid over as far as I could. By the time I was in, the dress was up to my thighs. Ben joined me, staring at my legs as I adjusted the dress, and then his stare settled on my chest. I glanced down quickly to make sure I hadn't popped out of the top. Nope. Everything was packed in nice and tight.

I smiled at Ben, but he didn't notice, because he was still staring at my chest. I coughed politely, drawing his attention to my face. He grinned sheepishly, and any annoyance I had evaporated. My breasts were sort of out there to be ogled, and of course Ben couldn't help but notice them. It was cute the way he blushed when he was caught.

"You clean up good, Davis."

I smiled, not sure what to say. Instead of using his nickname for me, he'd reverted to calling me by my last name, like Ryan and Justin did. It should have been a sign of how comfortable he was around me, but I wished he would use my first name. I didn't want him to see me like Ryan and Justin did. I wanted him to think of me as someone special.

"You look pretty good yourself."

Ben leaned forward and pressed his lips to mine. I gasped, and he plunged his tongue in my mouth. Surprised, my eyes widened, and I gripped his shoulders, not in delight but to stabilize him. I didn't want him falling on top of me. I tasted a hint of something sour on his breath. Tequila? Whiskey?

When I pushed to keep him from practically lying on top of me, he sat up.

"What's wrong?"

"Have you been drinking?"

He pressed a side panel, which popped out to reveal several small bottles of liquor. "It's a full bar, baby."

He'd shown up at my house to pick me up after having a cocktail or two? Was he insane?

As if reading my mind, he tried to reassure me. "Don't worry, I gargled some Listerine before I met your folks."

Well, hey, as long as you tried to hide the fact that you

were drinking from my folks, everything was hunky-dory.

Not.

"You're mad."

"Ya think?" I was never one for the clever retorts when I was pissed off. "If my dad suspected you'd been drinking, he never would have let me go tonight."

"He didn't figure it out, so what's the problem?"

I stared at him in dismay. Who was this guy? Did he have any idea how I would have felt after spending all that time and money to ready myself for a dance that I couldn't attend because my dad figured out my date was prefunctioning before picking me up?

I shook my head, trying to let my anger go. I didn't want to ruin this evening. Maybe I was being a bit of a prude. Justin partied on the weekends and before dances. Morgan never seemed to mind. In fact, she always had a drink or two herself.

"There's no problem. Just next time, could you wait to start the drinking until *after* you pick me up?"

"Next time, huh? I think you dig me, Davis." He smiled so sweetly that my anger sort of melted away. How fair was it that such a handsome face could melt my anger so quickly?

He leaned forward and kissed me gently this time. His lips were soft, and without his tongue, I couldn't taste the alcohol. It was more pleasant, more romantic.

He pulled away slightly, his sexy confidence in place like armor. "We'll take it slow, Spencer. We have all night."

I wasn't sure what to say. I wasn't sure what he *meant*. We had all night to be together? To get to know each other? Or was he alluding to something more? We had all night to fill in the blank? I wasn't sure, and I felt vulnerable being alone in the car with him. Luckily, the limo came to a halt at the next house on our stop, Morgan's.

Morgan had dyed her hair hot pink for the occasion. Well, not all her hair, just the top. Her natural dark brown color was pulled up in back. Justin wore a suit, and his shirt matched Morgan's new hair color perfectly. Even the handkerchief in the black jacket was hot pink. Morgan wore a black dress with spaghetti straps and a hot pink choker. Connected to the choker was the charm that Justin had made for her birthday.

Next stop was Alyssa's house, and my stomach kept clenching into knots. Who had she picked? Which guy would top the list tonight?

We entered her house in a cluster, everyone chatting and complimenting each other, when I recognized his voice. Alyssa's one-night stand was none other than Zachary Thames.

No way.

"Spencer!" Alyssa shrieked. "You look so great. I knew that dress was made for you!"

She grabbed my hand and admired my corsage. I tried very hard not to lose my cool. Through clenched teeth, I kept my voice down. "You're not serious about Zach, are you?"

She looked at me, eyes wide in innocence. "What do you mean?"

"You can't be thinking of using Zach this way."

"Using him? I would never use him. With Zach I can have full disclosure, which is a relief. And you shouldn't really care anyway, right? You're with Ben tonight."

We both looked over at Ben, talking with Justin and Morgan. Zach listened quietly but didn't contribute to the conversation.

"I care because Zach's my *friend*." I stressed the last word.

"I'm your friend too. Don't you trust me?"

"Implicitly, in all things except this goal of yours. I don't want Zach hurt."

She tried to reassure me with a smile. "Zach won't be hurt. I promise. It will all be up to him. If tonight works out like it should, then all of us will get what we want."

Ben caught my eye and winked in my direction. A shiver ran down my spine.

Everyone gets what they want?

Alyssa's mom took our pictures, directing us like a marine sergeant. She didn't bother using our names, even though she knew what they were. She just barked out instructions like "Pink girl, sit here. Gold boy, next to SoonYi."

We were all suffering from a classic case of the giggles by the time we headed back to the limo.

Zach grabbed my arm to get a moment alone with me as everyone piled into the car.

"Spencer, I want you to know that you literally took my breath away when I saw you tonight. You look every inch the Greek goddess."

I could tell by the way he held my gaze and looked into my eyes that he meant every word. His stare had swept over my entire dress when he first pulled me aside. Now they rested on my face, never once dipping lower to gape at my breasts. Zach was a class act.

"Thank you. And you look very handsome yourself. Alyssa's dress color really compliments you." I practically choked on the next words. "You make a really cute couple."

Zach opened his mouth to speak, but Alyssa called from inside the limo.

"Come on, slowpokes, we're running behind schedule."

We both moved forward. Zach stood to my right to help me inside the car and then slid in across from me. Billy slammed the door and we were off.

"Does anyone have any idea who Ryan asked?" Alyssa addressed the group.

There was a round of negative responses.

I looked over to Ben and found him staring down my top. Again. I nudged him with a frown.

"Sorry, can't help it. I had no idea how hot your body was under those sweatshirts."

I blushed. Zach glowered at Ben, and Alyssa looked strangely smug. It was going to be a long night.

We arrived at Ryan's place. The reason for all his secrecy became evident when we entered the Payne household. Standing next to him, in a designer dress that cost more than all our dresses combined, was none other than Shelby Grant.

"Oh, fu-uck me," Morgan said under her breath.

Exactly.

This was Ryan's chaos release. He wanted a catfight in the limo or something to appease his need for anarchy. Maybe he just wanted an easy lay. Ben and Justin high-fived him and razzed one another about their monkey suits. Zach joined them the minute he sensed the unease among the women. The girls eyed one another warily.

Alyssa was the first to speak. "You look very nice, Shelby."

"Thanks. It's a Stella McCartney."

When none of us oohed and aahed over this revelation (Stella who?), Mrs. Payne came to the rescue.

"Let's get everyone together for some photos."

Finally it was time to leave for dinner. Flash spots floated in my vision for several minutes before dissipating. By everyone else's dazed expression, I could tell they were suffering from the same effects.

Billy drove us to an upscale restaurant, where we were not alone as far as the Winter Formal crowd was concerned. Half the restaurant was dressed for the occasion, and pretty soon, everyone was just calling back and forth to one another.

Instead of being angry, the other patrons wore patient smiles, and I saw more than one woman gaze nostalgically at the gowns on parade.

The boys, being bottomless pits, ordered steak and anything fried. Alyssa and I had the pasta, and Morgan ate the salmon. Shelby had a salad. And it was a side salad at that.

I got up to use the restroom, and to my surprise, Shelby joined me. We stood in front of the mirror to reapply our lipstick and check for food particles in our teeth. I had to ask, "Aren't you still hungry?"

She blotted her nose with a special tissue and shrugged indifferently. "I'm used to it."

Standing next to Shelby in the bathroom filled me with

a different sensation from standing next to Alyssa. When I stood next to Alyssa, I felt like a giant. Shelby and I were basically the same height, and standing next to her made me feel like I was watching one of those "Save the starving kids" infomercials. I felt like I should force-feed her a sandwich.

Her skin was stretched over her bones, and I could actually count her ribs across her chest beneath the metal green material. Her dress was short and done in the balloon skirt style, which only really skinny people can pull off anyway. I wondered how her stick legs could hold up her weight.

"I couldn't do it," I murmured, shaking my head.

She turned to me and smirked. "Obviously."

She left me standing in the middle of the bathroom with my mouth hanging open. What nerve! Suddenly the oddest thing happened. Instead of feeling inferior and embarrassed about my size, I took a long look at myself in the mirror and stood up taller.

Sure, I wasn't an Ana or a Mia like her, but I was wearing a beautiful gown that made me feel like a goddess, and I was being escorted by the guy Shelby wanted and couldn't get.

I laughed, feeling liberated. She couldn't take this evening away from me. It was mine. I swiped some more gloss on my lips and strolled out of the bathroom, humming a little tune. I was really looking forward to the dance. Nothing Shelby Grant could say tonight would ruin it.

chapter

18

Winter Formal was being
held at the Embassy Suites Hotel. It was the only hotel in
town large enough to accommodate a function of this size.

Since we had the limo and our driver was a friend, the
party started inside the cavernous vehicle. I'm not a drinker,
and tonight was no exception.

"Come on, Davis, one drink. Quit playing it so safe and
loosen up a little." Ben offered me a glass for the umpteenth
time, and I refused.

"Why don't you double-dog dare her, and she'll really have
to do it then," Zach suggested with a hint of sarcasm.

Ben smiled tightly and stopped offering me drinks. I smiled at Zach in gratitude. After half the Crew had a couple of drinks in them, we headed inside. Billy would be watching a movie in the back while waiting for us.

When everyone had gotten out of the limo, the girls arranged their dresses, adjusted their bodices, and made sure they had their purses. The guys put their suit coats back on, and we made our way through the parking lot.

The dance hall was ablaze with hundreds of twinkling lights, flashing lasers, pounding music, and an ice sculpture.

"Bet you five bucks it's already spiked," Ryan said, looking at the clock. I couldn't believe it was ten thirty. Ben had picked me up at seven this evening. Where had all the time gone?

We piled our purses, wraps, and any coats the guys didn't want to wear onto a table, staking our claim. We flooded onto the dance floor. No one really danced with anyone in particular. We were one gyrating organism, having fun and getting down to the music.

The music abruptly changed. The soft chords of a love ballad began while Zach and I were facing each other. Both of us were breathing hard, flushed from the exertion, when Ben grabbed my hand from behind and turned me around.

"Finally I get to hold you in my arms."

Ben swept me close, and we swayed with the music. I put

my head on his shoulder because it was easier than trying to hold it upright when he held me so tightly. This was it. This should have been the most magical night of my life. Why wasn't I overcome with joy at being in Benjamin's arms?

I looked over his shoulder and saw Alyssa gliding across the dance floor with Zach. She was chatting and he was smiling. They looked totally natural and comfortable in each other's arms. Alyssa was well on the way to achieving her goal. I sighed in resignation.

Ben misunderstood my sigh and started stroking my back with his hands. It wasn't unpleasant. Almost hypnotic. His hand touching my bare back, his thumb trailing circular patterns as his other hand moved lower and lower . . . I felt his rock-hard thighs against mine, and maybe something else as well. What was the old joke? Is that a gun in your pocket or are you just glad to see me?

I tried to wiggle away, but Ben held me tight.

I looked back over at Zach and found him staring at me, his lips in a thin line. I smiled at him, but he didn't return the gesture and instead leaned his ear down to Alyssa's lips so he could hear what she was saying. A boiling inferno filled my stomach and threatened to erupt from my throat when Zach brought his hand to Alyssa's face and brushed an errant strand of hair from her cheek.

Serena Robar

I felt a slight breeze across my ear and tried to shrug the sensation away. It took a moment to realize that it was Ben, blowing in my ear. His lips touched my lobe, and I felt his tongue dance along the edge. I should have been ecstatic, overcome with passion and desire. So why did I feel so annoyed that he couldn't keep his hands to himself? And what was up with all this swaying-in-a-circle crap? Zach was moving all across the dance floor, and I couldn't see what they were doing at this moment.

My heart started to hammer in my chest. I couldn't do this. I couldn't be with Ben when all I could do was think of Zach. When did this happen? When had I fallen out of lust with Ben and into . . . what exactly with Zach?

I needed air. I had to get away. The song seemed to go on forever. I felt my body tremble with the urge to break free and run. Ben held me even tighter, and I was suffocating. I was drowning in his nearness, and all I wanted to do was escape.

"Bathroom," I gasped. "I have to go now!" I broke away from him as the song's last chords played out. He looked surprised at my sudden departure, but I didn't care. I couldn't breathe. I had to get away *right now*.

My best bet was to disappear outside into the cool night air, but I didn't want everyone in the lobby seeing me flee into the darkness. Instead I headed for the restroom and ran to the farthest stall in the back. I locked it, put down the lid, and sat, holding my head between my legs.

I took oxygen deeply into my lungs. I needed air. My vision swam in front of my eyes. Deep breath. Again.

The door burst open to admit some girls from the dance. I couldn't see them and they couldn't see me, so I ignored the interruption for the most part.

"So, Shelby, how was the limo ride over here? Get into any catfights?"

I froze on the toilet. Marissa was addressing her queen.

"Nah, she was hardly going to make a scene, and besides, I doubt she has any idea."

"Ben sure does look hot tonight. I can't believe he's here with Spencer Davis, blech." I thought it was Kristi's voice, but I couldn't be sure.

"Oh, yeah, you should have been at dinner with them. She ate everything on her plate and then finished his."

They gasped. "No way! For real?"

"I swear."

That wasn't true! I hadn't even finished my meal, and Ben ate the rest of it after he'd polished off his steak. What a lying bitch!

"I mean, I sat across from her at dinner, and she was making moon eyes at Ben. She has no idea we've been having sex for weeks. Pathetic, really."

"Are you two going to go out?" Kristi asked.

"Hardly. The boy's a player. I like what we have right now. No strings attached. Besides, I'm here with Ryan, and I'm thinking it's time to try a new flavor."

They all laughed and left the bathroom together. I couldn't move. I was literally frozen to the seat of the toilet. If the fire alarm went off right now, I wouldn't be able to move. They'd find my charred corpse still sitting atop the crapper. I heard water drip in the sink.

Drip.

Drip.

Drip.

I was such an idiot. I did his lab experiments, his homework—and I even gave him the Hostess cupcake from my lunch bag. And he was fucking Shelby Grant!

What a prize fool I was. I'd even started taking the Pill for him, thinking he was the One. That he was worthy of such a significant gift as my virginity.

My brain backpedaled. "Consider the source of the gossip," it said to me. "Shelby's poisonous tongue isn't known for telling the truth."

She hadn't known I was in the bathroom. What did she gain by telling her friends about Ben? Would she do it to save face? Hardly—she was here with Ryan. Ryan Payne was the trump card to Benjamin.

I stood up and paced the stall. Whether it was true or not didn't seem to matter, since I'd discovered I was harboring deeper feelings for Zach.

How could I have felt so certain about Benjamin just weeks ago? And now the thought of Alyssa touching Zach made my stomach hurt.

I needed someone to talk to, but who? Alyssa was my go-to girl. I couldn't exactly go to her about this, could I? No, I needed Morgan. I stared at the scuffed tiles and dingy grout on the floor. I would have to leave the bathroom. My feet refused to cooperate. I couldn't hide in the bathroom all night. Eventually my date would wonder what happened to me.

Maybe he would leave with someone else? My heart swelled with hope. Wait a minute. I should be devastated at the thought of Ben leaving with someone else. Instead I felt relieved. It was the thought of Zach leaving with Alyssa, knowing her master plan, that devastated me. There was no comparison.

I unlocked the stall door and practically sprinted out the door, surprising some girls as they tried to enter the bathroom.

"Sorry," I apologized, zipping past them. I slowed my pace down to a brisk walk, trying not to draw attention to myself. Look for pink. Look for pink. Egads, everyone had on pink tonight. WTF? Where was the pink hair? Where was Morgan?

I entered the dance hall from a side door, hoping Ben wouldn't see me. I crept slowly along the wall behind the ice sculpture. Lots of freshmen were drinking from the punch, so I assumed it had managed to get spiked.

I was getting closer to our table. Where was Ben? Was he dancing? Wait a minute. What was going on by the other set of doors? A flash of pink. Ah, Morgan. Jackpot. I caught sight of her and made a beeline. A commotion to her right grabbed my attention, and I turned just in time to see Zach take a swing at Ben. *Bammo!*

Ben staggered back and returned the favor. Whereas Zach had hit Ben in the jaw, Ben punched Zach in the nose. It was like someone had turned on a faucet, and blood poured out. I was rooted to the spot until Ben laughed. Ben was going to take another swing, but Zach couldn't see for all the blood. I was filled with a rage I'd never known before. Ben was hurting Zach, and there was no way I was going to let that continue. I ran between them.

"Stop it!" I pushed Ben's chest with some serious force, and he rocked back a step.

"What are you doing? He started it!"

I glared at him. "Ben, you are *such* an asshole."

chapter 19

I *turned toward Zach,*
yanking one of my scarves out of its bracelet and cramming it
under Zach's nose to help staunch the bleeding. He balked.

"What?" I demanded, pulling the scarf away from his
mouth so I could hear him.

"Get away, I'm getting blood all over you."

I looked down at my beautiful Grecian gown, and sure
enough, spots of blood were splashed across my chest.

"Whatever." I maneuvered him back toward a chair so he
could sit down and tilted his head back. The Crew rushed to
our side to help out. Actually, Morgan and Alyssa wanted to

help; Ryan and Justin wanted to re-enact the argument, blow by blow.

"What happened?" I snapped at Ryan, who was laughing his ass off.

"Don't know. I was just standing there, and the next minute Zach spun Ben around and clocked him."

"Why? Why would you do that?" I pinched Zach's nose a little harder than I should, and he yelped.

"Sorry," I muttered. "Morgan, get me some ice wrapped in a napkin. That should help with the bleeding."

"I'll get some ice for Ben, in case he needs it." Alyssa scurried to follow Morgan. Like I cared if Ben needed ice. He could swell up like the Elephant Man for all I cared.

Where were the chaperones for this affair? There was a fight in the middle of the dance and not one of them was here to break it up.

Zach tried to stand up, but I forced him down. "Oh no, you don't. You sit until this nose clots. Of all the stupid, irresponsible things to do, Zach. I can't believe you started a fight. And with Ben, of all people. What were you thinking?"

He pressed his lips together, refusing to answer. But eventually he had to open his mouth to gasp for air, since his nose was blocked, making breathing problematic.

I dropped down to one knee so we were eye level. Keeping

one hand on the scarf beneath his nose and the other on the side of his face, I checked under his eye to see if it was going to blacken.

"Was it worth it? Did you think for one minute how I would feel?" He tried to look away, but I held his nose firm.

Morgan returned with some ice wrapped in a napkin. I traded it for the scarf and let Zach hold it against his nose. He winced, but kept it in place.

"I should go home," he said.

I nodded my head in agreement. "Absolutely."

I turned away from him. "Morgan, I can't find Ben or Alyssa. Could you tell them we left? I'll send the limo back to you guys so you have a ride home."

"Sure thing." She hugged me. "I don't think anything is gonna top this."

I made my way back toward our table and picked up my purse. Zach followed me to the table.

"You don't have to leave," he objected.

I looked down at my blood-spattered dress. "Yeah, I really kind of do."

"I'm so sorry, Spencer. I'll pay for cleaning it. I swear."

"I'm not worried about it, Zach. Come on. Let's go."

"Don't you want to say good night to your date?" he asked stiffly.

"Not particularly." His brow furrowed. I'd confused him.

If Billy was surprised we were leaving early and ditching our dates at the dance, he didn't comment. Inside the limo it was nice and toasty.

"I guess I ruined your night, huh?" Zach hung his head low.

I snorted in response, looking out the window.

"Hey, you didn't have to leave. A little blood on your dress wouldn't stop Ben. As a matter of fact, I'm sure he'd be more than willing to help you out of it."

I raised an eyebrow at his tone. Zach was pissed off.

"You punched my date out and you're mad at *me*?"

I remembered how annoying it was to keep removing Benjamin's hands from my ass and move my neck farther away when he wanted to blow in my ear. All I wanted to do was try to see what Zach was doing, and now he was mad at me! That was rich.

"Your date is a dick!"

"True," I agreed, and looked back out the window.

"He—what?"

"He's a dick. You're right. But he could have really hurt you."

"Like you'd care." Zach pouted.

"You have no idea how much I'd care!" I declared angrily. "And that's a problem, isn't it? I care. I care way too much!"

My voice rose and he answered in kind. "Yeah, well, maybe seeing him put his hands all over you wasn't exactly a picnic for me, either."

"Yeah? How about you dancing cheek-to-cheek with Alyssa all night? Huh?"

"Are you yelling at me because you like me?" His voice was incredulous.

"No, you idiot. I'm yelling at you because I think I love you. And I'm not happy about it!"

Zach's eyes widened in shock. I glared at him with a mutinous expression on my face.

"Have you ever thought about us, in this way, before?" I asked him.

He took a moment to think before replying.

"No, not until recently. For some reason, seeing you with Ben made me so angry. I couldn't stand the thought of him touching you or"—his voice cracked—"kissing you."

I nodded. "Me too. I mean, I hated seeing your arms around Alyssa at the dance tonight."

"Really?" His voice betrayed his delight.

I chuckled. "Really. It's just we've been friends so long, I'm wondering if we could ever move past that. I'm worried that kissing you would be like kissing a brother."

"You think of me as a brother?" He was incredulous.

"I—I really don't know. This is very confusing."

"Then let me clear things up for you."

His hands moved up to cup my face as I leaned into him. I couldn't say for sure whose lips touched whose first, but there wasn't any hesitancy or reluctance. He was confident and at ease taking my lips into his possession. The kiss was perfectly orchestrated with desire and intent. His lips were firm and yielding. I gasped when his tongue swept into my mouth and gently touched mine. His hands captured the nape of my neck when he deepened the kiss.

My hands trembled, and I clutched the front of his jacket to steady them. Holy crap! This was *not* what it was like to kiss a brother. This was hot and sweet and tremendous and terrifying and brilliant, all at once and immediately. He tasted like peppermint Life Savers, my favorite, and when he pulled away slightly I made a whimper of protest that didn't last, because he took my lower lip between his teeth and sucked gently.

This was what all the fuss was about. It wasn't the same sensations I experienced with Ben on the couch. Zach was making me feel hot and anxious, and I wanted more. More of his kisses, more of his hands, more of every vibration coming alive in my body. No, this wasn't a crush, and these feelings weren't being delivered by the fertile soccer star at our school. This storm of sensation was manifested by the "nice guy," the breakup wingman, my best friend. I wanted to laugh at every girl who'd ever looked at Zach as tame.

He pulled away again, slowly, leisurely, until our lips barely touched. I was panting, which was a little embarrassing, until I noticed Zach was as well.

"Still feel sisterly toward me?"

"God, no!" I gasped.

His lips trailed kisses toward my ear, his cheek slid across mine. The scratchy whiskers felt rough against my skin, but I liked the sensation. I'd never felt so grateful to my sister for insisting I go jewelry-less when Zach's teeth grazed my earlobe. His breath was warm and sent delicious shivers down my spine.

"Mmm, you smell good," Zach murmured, inhaling my perfume. I vaguely remembered moving my arms around his neck and digging them into his thick hair. His breath tickled my skin until his tongue traced the edge of my ear and I moaned. Dear Lord, I actually moaned. How slutty was that?

"Zach?" I gasped softly.

"Hmm?" He continued to nuzzle my ear.

"Billy's not watching us, is he?"

We both sort of froze at that thought. At least our reaction proved that neither of us was into exhibitionism. Zach lifted his head toward the privacy glass and muttered something under his breath that sounded like "pervert," but I could have been mistaken. Billy had cracked the window and was watching us make out through his rearview mirror.

Zach smacked the glass and barked for Billy to take us home. Billy just grinned like an idiot and shut his window.

Even though the tinted glass was up, we were both too paranoid to continue where we'd left off. Luckily, Zach lived very close, and we were at his home in no time. We told Billy to go back and pick up the others. Zach promised to drive me home later, and suddenly we were alone again.

The house was dark and we tried to be quiet, not wanting to disturb anyone. Max lifted his head up when we opened the door. After a brief tail wag, he snuggled deeper into his dog pillow and went back to sleep.

Zach shook his head ruefully. "Someday we're going to be ax-murdered in our beds and Max will have slept through it. I'm gonna run upstairs and change. I'll be right back."

He took the stairs two at a time, and I opened my purse to text my sister. My curfew was one a.m., but now that I was at Zach's house, I figured I could hang a little longer.

LEFT DANCE, AT ZACHS, TELL MOM.

Short, sweet, and to the point. A moment later my phone chirped.

Zach rejoined me, carrying some sweats and a tee.

"I thought you might want to change. You don't have to …"

I snatched the clothes from his hands and hurried to the bathroom. It was heaven removing my sandals. I imagined my feet would have hurt a thousand times more if I'd tried to wear a stiletto heel like Shelby.

I unzipped my dress and shimmied out of it. Next I wrestled with my body armor (aka Spanx) and felt so much better once I was free of it. Left in panties and a bra, I pulled on Zach's sweats. Ahh, so comfy. I rolled them up several times so I wouldn't trip and pulled a Pirate Beaver tee over my head.

Opening the bathroom door, I tiptoed out barefoot, with shoes and dress in hand. Zach had anticipated my needs and had a paper bag waiting for me on the kitchen table. I joined him in the living room, where he left the lights off. Only the glow from the kitchen illuminated the room. Very cozy.

"Can you help me with my hair?"

"Sure, what do I do?"

I pulled up a section. "I need to unclip the pearls and take out all the bobby pins."

"Piece of cake."

Five minutes later he was cursing under his breath. "How many pins do you have in there, anyway?"

We freed the last of my hair, and I rubbed my hands over my scalp. "Ahh, that feels so much better."

Zach replaced my hands with his and started to massage. He gently ran his fingers through my hair without making tangles or pulling snags.

"You are so *good* at this," I couldn't help the groan that escaped my lips.

"Comes from years of scratching Max in all the right places."

I was sitting cross-legged between his legs. I smacked his knee for comparing me to the dog.

"Ow."

Zach continued his massage, dropping his hands lower and rubbing my neck and shoulders, then going back up into my hair. I was melting under his fingers.

"Why did you punch Ben?" His fingers paused momentarily, and then went back to massaging.

"I didn't like what he said."

"Which was?"

Silence.

"Why won't you tell me?"

"Because I overreacted. I should have made a smart-ass

comment to defuse the situation, but instead I, well, I pun-ched him."

"So you're embarrassed that you hit him."

"No, I'm not. He deserved it. I regret *losing control* and punching him. Not the punching itself."

"Ah." I totally didn't get it.

We were silent for a few more moments. I tried to think of what Ben could have said to make Zach lose control like that.

Bingo.

"He said something about me, didn't he?"

Zach didn't confirm or deny, but his hands dug deeper.

"What did he say about me, Zach? I have a right to know."

Zach blew out a sigh and stopped rubbing my shoulders. I got up and sat next to him on the coach.

"He showed the guys a key card to a hotel room and said he was taking someone's virginity tonight."

"Oh." I didn't know what else to say. Just "Oh."

"Yeah, so before I knew it I'd spun him around and punched."

I gave him a teasing little smile. "You were defending my honor, Zach. That's sweet."

He grabbed my upper arms and pulled me closer. "No, I wasn't, Spencer. I punched him because the thought of anyone else touching your skin makes me insane. No one should have the right to kiss you and taste you but me. I punched him because he wanted to take something that was rightfully mine. Your first time should be my first time. So there it is. That's the reason I punched him."

He looked ready to flinch at my reaction. Did he think I was going to rant and rave at his gall? Hell, no. What he'd just said was the single most romantic thing any guy had ever said or done. And that included Justin's painted-ass message to Morgan.

"I feel the same way, Zach. I feel the *exact* same way."

He had approximately one second to register what I said before I threw myself into his arms and onto his lips. He held me while we kissed for what seemed like an eternity. His kisses were so insistent, yet tender. It was like his lips were convincing me of the rightness of the situation. He was evangelizing me into seeing we belonged together.

His hands roamed my back and hair. I ran my hands over his shoulders (they were so broad) and down his back. He pressed me back onto the couch and covered his body with mine. It felt so right to have his weight on me.

"Spencer?" His voice was raspy and strained.

"Yes," I moaned in response.

"I love the way you taste and feel under me. And I don't

want you to think for a minute that I don't want you, 'cause it should be fairly apparent that I do. It's just, this is so new and I want, well, I want to savor it. I want to explore it and dissect it and relish it. I don't want to rush it."

He echoed the thoughts in my heart exactly. Zach was my best friend, but now our relationship was taking on a whole new dynamic, and I wanted to slow down and discover all the little things about him as a boyfriend.

I nodded my head in agreement. "I know, Zach. I feel the same way. I want to wait. I want to savor this new getting-to-know-each-other period too."

He gave a shaky laugh. "This could very well kill me."

My hand was shaking as I reached up to caress his face. "Then we'll die together."

He grabbed my hand and brought it to his lips and kissed each fingertip. "You're so worth the wait, Spencer."

My eyes filled with tears. I was moved by the depth of emotion behind his declaration. "You too, Zach, you too."

I went to bed with swollen lips and a huge grin on my face. I woke up with chapped lips and a dreamy smile on my face. Being around Zach made me feel that good. Heidi ran into my room and jumped on the bed.

"Get up, sleepyhead. Tell me all about it. Give me the juicy details."

She dropped down onto her butt next to me with expectant eyes. Where to begin?

"How did you end up at Zach's?"

"I sort of ditched my date and left with Zach."

"Really?" Her eyes were wide. "I'm impressed."

"Impressed how?"

"Impressed that you finally figured out that you and Zach belong together. I swear you two were the only ones on the planet who couldn't see it."

I could have argued and denied my feelings. Instead I let a huge smile emerge that said everything I could never say.

Heidi eyed me with fascination. "Really? That good, huh?"

"Zach is a perfect gentleman," I assured her, but added wickedly, "and, oh yeah, it's that good."

"I'm happy for you, sis, really happy. Now get up and get dressed, 'cause Alyssa's downstairs waiting for you."

She bounded out of the room before I could ask her if Alyssa seemed upset. First I went to the dance with the boy she liked, and then I left the dance with her date. No one was that understanding.

I changed out of Zach's clothes with reluctance. I wanted to wear them all day because they smelled like him. And not that funky corn-chip boy smell. A clean, fresh scent that was probably fabric softener, but I associated it with Zach.

I went from boys' sweats to girls' sweats in less than a minute. Fishing for a ponytail holder, I gathered my rat's nest and shoved it into the elastic. When I couldn't delay the inevitable any longer, I made my way downstairs.

Serena Robar

Alyssa was laughing with my mom and sister, regaling them with stories about the dance. She watched me enter the room and finished up her latest story, saying, "And Spencer would know all this if she hadn't stolen my date and left the dance."

I winced, but Alyssa laughed after she said it. She didn't look upset. Actually, she seemed to be in a pretty good mood.

"Let's go upstairs," I suggested, and led the way back to my room.

"So what happened after I left?" I asked.

"Who cares about that? I want to know what happened between you and Zach."

That grin of unbridled happiness burst forth again, and Alyssa squealed loudly. "I knew it! I knew it. You two hooked up."

"We're exploring this new phase in our relationship. We're taking our time."

"But you did kiss him, right?"

"Hell, yeah," I assured her.

"Phew! You had me worried for a second." She took my hand in hers. "You're happy about this, right? You don't regret leaving Ben at the dance?"

"You know, I should feel bad about ditching him, but I really don't. As soon as I saw Zach get hurt, it was like I knew, ya know? I knew he was the One."

"Wow, that's amazing. You two crazy kids were made for each other."

"Enough about me. What happened with you? I tried to tell you I was taking Zach home, but I couldn't find you. Was Ben mad that I left him there?"

Alyssa chewed on her lower lip a moment. "Actually, no. He wasn't pissed. He found, uh, comfort in another's arms."

"Oh. So Shelby got her man after all, huh?"

"No, not Shelby."

She wouldn't look me in the face.

"Omigod! It was you! You hooked up with Ben."

"You did leave with Zach."

"Don't worry, Alyssa, I'm hardly mad. I'm just sort of flabbergasted. How'd it happen?"

"I told you before, Spencer. The characters might change but the goal stayed the same. He had a room key but needed a girl, since his date had left him. I needed a guy, since my date left me. It was easy math."

"So you did it, then? You slept with him?"

She shrugged like it was no big deal.

"How do you feel about it? Are you okay?"

She walked around the room. "Actually, I feel relieved that it's over and done with. I can stop obsessing about it now."

"Does this mean Ben is going to tell everyone you put out?"

She shrugged again. "I don't know. I mean, I assumed he would, but he was all clingy and emotional after it was over. He kept telling me that no one understood him like I did. That we were good together, yada, yada, yada. Frankly, it creeped me out a little."

"Oh, no. You've been body snatched by love-'em-and-leave-'em Ryan Payne."

She ignored the jab. "So, get dressed so we can play some Guitar Hero at Ryan's."

"Really? You want to do that?" I don't know what I was thinking would happen. I thought she might want to talk about it or something, but she just looked at me funny.

"Why wouldn't I? Oh, you mean because Ben might be there?" She shrugged. "He told me he couldn't go to Ryan's for a while. I guess he snuck out when he was grounded and got busted. The only reason they let him go to the dance was because he took you."

"Oh." I guess doing Shelby Grant did have a price, after all. "Then give me just a second and we can go."

I grabbed some socks and followed Alyssa downstairs to get my shoes. I told Mom where we were headed, pulled them on, and headed toward the door. On the porch was a large poster board, folded in half. On the front, two stick figures were enclosed in a heart, holding hands. One had curly hair, so I assumed that one was me.

"I found it taped to your door this morning when I came over. I think it's for you."

Inside was another limerick from the Mysterious Poet. I read it aloud, and we laughed.

"He rhymed 'celibacy' with 'wait and see,'" Alyssa noted, her eyes watering from laughing so hard. "What a nut."

"Yeah," I said, hugging the card to my chest. "But he's my nut. All mine."

We arrived at Ryan's, and each of us took our traditional places in the media room, with one small exception. I sat on Zach's lap while Ryan and Justin played the first round. It felt so right to cuddle with him, like we'd been doing it forever, yet at the same time, it was new and exciting. The Crew kept making gagging sounds whenever we kissed, but I didn't care.

Sometimes the new guy is what you want, and sometimes it's the jock. In my case it was both. But if you're really, really lucky, the guy you want ends up being your best friend.

Supersecret Author Confessions

For those of you who have read my previous books, you know I try to add an Easter egg at the end of each story. And if you're new to my books, be sure to pick up my backlist. I dish about my worst date ever, my first published work at age six entitled "Ode to Fish," and much, much more.

I get a lot of mail from readers wanting to know where I get the inspiration for my stories. How did they come about? This Supersecret Author Confession will reveal what events in *Giving Up the V* actually happened to me or someone I know. Fasten your seat belts, here we go.

1. Spencer's first visit to an ob-gyn was my first visit to an ob-gyn in college. Previously, my doctors had all been women, and this was the first time I was going to be seen by a male doctor. I was very nervous. When I met him, I nearly fell off the table because he looked exactly like my mom's boss. They, of course, were not the same person, but it was freaky all the same. And the WD-40 comment? Word for word what happened at my visit. And the mirror? Bingo! He offered that to me as well.

2. A quick shout-out to my teenage cousins Sydney, Cheyenne, and Tiara, who love my books. I immortalized your names in this one, ladies. Enjoy.

3. The pregnancy-test-in-an-open-purse scenario. This didn't happen to me, but my best friend's daughter was telling us how a girl at her school put a pregnancy test in her purse because she was desperate for attention. I thought the story was very telling about high school today, and also very sad. I wanted to use it, but I didn't want Alyssa to come off as pathetic. I liked that she was empowered because it was all part of her "devirginization" plan.

4. Devirginization: I wanted to coin my own term. Who hasn't heard of truthiness? I adore Stephen Colbert and think I'd make a great guest for his show. I sent him a copy of *Giving Up the V* with this passage highlighted. I'm still waiting to hear from his people. I'm sure they will be calling any day now. Or issuing a restraining order.

5. Bare-ass love message to Morgan: I don't know of anyone who has done this, but how cool would that be? So my challenge to you, dear reader, is: Confess your love to someone in an unusual fashion. Nothing says love quite like total strangers baring their ass with a message. Hallmark, beware.

6. "You can stop jiggling now." My hand to God, this happened to me when I was a junior in high school. I was changing into my gym clothes, and a senior girl whose locker was close to mine looked over and said, "You can stop jiggling now" when I did a little hop to pull up my shorts. Oh, yeah. She totally did. I remember it like it was yesterday. What. A. Bitch. (You thought I was going to talk about forgiveness and moving on, didn't you? Hah!)

7. The Mysterious Poet. I stole this story from my husband. When he liked a girl in high school, he would leave her little notes, poems, or flowers from M.R., or Mysterious Romantic. Not once did this pay off. They never could figure out who M.R. really was. This goes to show that the nice guy rarely finishes first, except in my book. Zach is romantic, charming, and old-fashioned, but he knows how to lead when the situation calls for it. Yummy.

8. Cotton the terrier. That is my dog. You can see pictures of him on my website, as well as discover other Supersecret Confessions at www.serenarobar.com.

So that's it, folks. I hope you enjoyed reading *Giving Up the V* as much as I enjoyed writing it. Be sure to keep an eye out for my next release.

—Serena Robar

About the Author

Serena Robar spent her high school days addicted to reading romances of all kinds. She would tuck a romance novel in her open science book and pretend to be following along with the class when she was really lost in a fantasy world of happily ever after. Though her knowledge of mitochondria is woefully limited, she boasts a vast array of trivia about the pirate trade of the sixteenth century, American pioneer life, and Regency etiquette of the Ton.

Serena lives in the Pacific Northwest and has been known to plot while laying down on the couch with her eyes shut. You can find her on the Web at www.serenarobar.com or friend her on Facebook or MySpace.

LET YOUR SCHOOL SPIRIT SHINE!
Winter Varsity Cheerleading
Call-Out Meeting
Wednesday
3:15
Cafeteria
Go Panthers!!!!!

I t is a truth universally acknowledged that a high school
boy in possession of great athletic ability must be in
want of . . .

A bowl of oatmeal.

At least on a cold November morning in Minnesota. And
maybe a carton of orange juice on the side, but definitely not
a girlfriend. Jack Paulson, mega basketball star and crush
extraordinaire, did not date. Just ask any girl in the Prairie
Stone High School junior class. The cheerleaders, the preps,
the drama queens, the band crew, the art nerds, the skater
chicks, the stoners, the loners, the freaks, the cool and the not-
so-cool, all of them had tried.

Including me.

I was hoping to try again that day, if only my best friend, Moni, would show up already. Ever since her parents divorced and her dad moved to Minneapolis, it was like he took Moni's punctuality with him. She'd been totally unreliable. So I wondered, could I pull it off? Could a lone geek girl linger by the cafeteria door in a casual manner? Not likely. You see, every school has a danger zone. At Prairie Stone, ours occupied the space in the lobby that was an equal distance between the cafeteria, the gym, and the girls' bathroom. It was the spot where all the popular kids hung out. A place the rest of us tried to avoid. Moni and I called it the gauntlet.

We discovered that term last year, in word origins class. In case you're wondering, *gauntlet (noun) = a form of punishment where the victim must endure suffering from many sources at the same time.* It comes from the Swedish word *gatlopp.* In Sweden, apparently, they used to punish reprobates *(n. those who are predestined to damnation)* by making them strip to the waist and then run between rows of soldiers who were armed with sticks and knotted ropes.

That sounded about right.

And so I stood at the edge of Prairie Stone's gauntlet, close enough to the gym to sniff the delicate aroma of sweaty socks, near enough to the cafeteria to catch a whiff of oatmeal—and the promise of Jack Paulson. One more step and I would officially enter gauntlet girl territory.

Chantal Simmons, the queen of cool and gatekeeper of popularity at PSHS, stood at the apex of it all. She turned her head in my direction, her blond hair flowing in a way rarely seen outside of shampoo commercials. Her glance made me consider climbing the stairs to the balcony and crossing over the top instead of pressing my way through—but only a coward would do that.

Which is to say, I've done it plenty.

Chantal had a radar for weakness. One wrong move and she'd find yours and use it against you. Forget those sticks and knotted ropes. Chantal could annihilate the hopes and dreams of your average high school junior with just a whisper. And once upon a time, back in the dark ages of childhood and middle school, Chantal Simmons was someone I had told all my secrets to. In retrospect, that was kind of like arming a rogue nation with a nuclear bomb.

No risk, no reward, I told myself. If I wanted an early-morning glimpse of Jack Paulson (and I did, I really, really did), then I needed to cross into enemy territory. Alone. But before I could step over that invisible boundary, someone called my name. Someone short, with a mass of yellow corkscrew curls poking out beneath a QTπ cap.

"Bethany!" My best friend, Moni Fredrickson, bounded up to me, still in her winter jacket, her cheeks pink from cold and her glasses fogged. "Brian just called me on my cell," she said. "They're in the Little Theater. They have Krispy Kremes. Brian said he'd save us one each, but you know how that works."

Of course I did. It is another truth universally acknowledged, that high school nerds in possession of a great number of Krispy Kremes must be in want of . . .

Nothing.

At least not until they shook out the last bit of sugary glaze from the box. Then it was total *Lord of the Flies* time while they searched for more. We had to get there before they tore Brian limb from limb. Moni pulled me along toward the Little Theater and away from the gauntlet. I glanced over my shoulder, sure Chantal was still glaring at me.

But she wasn't. No one was. Not a single gauntlet girl or wannabe peered in my direction. Instead they'd all turned toward the cafeteria, eyes fixed on a tall, retreating figure— one with dark spiky hair and a Prairie Stone High letter jacket. Jack Paulson. He didn't look back at me—not that I expected him to. But then, he didn't acknowledge Chantal, either.

Jack Paulson = Totally Girlproof.

I stumbled along behind Moni and wondered, *What would a girl have to do to get a boy like that to notice her?*

If there was such a thing as gauntlet girl territory at Prairie Stone, then the Little Theater was dork domain. Chantal Simmons might rule the lobby, but a few steps down the hall Todd Emerson (president of the chess club, co-captain of the debate team, editor of the school paper, and all-around boy genius) maintained a benevolent dictatorship over the academic superstars and the techies.

In other words, a bossier boy never lived.

Todd was Harvard bound. Or Yale bound. Well, certainly *somewhere* bound. Somewhere that was far snootier than (what I was sure he already thought of as) his humble beginnings. He was one of those kids who wouldn't return for a school reunion until he managed to make a billion dollars or overthrow a minor country.

A bright purple and gold notice hung on the door to the theater, instructing all who entered to LET YOUR SCHOOL SPIRIT SHINE! and inviting us to attend a call-out meeting for the winter varsity cheerleading squad. As if. I passed through the doorway, gripped the handrail, and followed Moni down the small flight of steps, my eyes adjusting to the semidarkness.

The Little Theater had killer acoustics, something Todd took advantage of up on the stage.

"Can you believe they denied Carlson's request for new desktop publishing software?" he thundered. "You know what they—" Todd broke off mid-rant. "Hey, Reynolds, how long does it take you to lay out the newspaper every month?"

I tried not to roll my eyes about the newspaper—or about Todd calling me by my last name. It was this thing he did, like I was a rookie reporter to his big-city editor in chief.

How long did it take for me to lay out the newspaper? "A while," I said. *Forever* was a better answer, but Todd was wound up enough. The computers we used were ancient, the software even older. I sometimes thought that cutting and pasting— with real scissors and glue—might be faster. Mr. Carlson, the journalism teacher, had been lobbying for upgrades for years.

"Guess what they bought instead?" said Todd. He gestured wildly from the podium. "Come on. Just guess."

I heard the sound of someone's stomach rumbling and the barest click of a Nintendo DS. I looked around at the collection of smarty-pants misfits that made up our "clique." These were the kids who lived to raise their hands in class. That no one offered a guess was a testament to the power Todd wielded over the group.

He pounded the lectern. The crack of his fist against wood echoed through the theater.

"They bought new"—Todd stepped out from behind the podium for effect—"*pom-poms.*" A look of disgust rolled across his face as he approached the front of the stage. "For the varsity *cheerleading* squad."

I glanced at Moni. She crossed her eyes at me and pointed toward the seat that held the Krispy Kreme box. Todd glared, daring someone, anyone, to speak.

A throat cleared behind us. "Well, I highly approved of the new outfits last year." This was Brian McIntyre, Todd's side-kick, mellow where Todd was high-strung, soft-spoken where Todd was loud. Brian was one of those boys whose looks froze in fourth grade. He had a roundish face and full cheeks, with sweet blue eyes and hair that flopped over his forehead. People constantly underestimated him, which was why he cleaned up in debate, at chess, and in the Math League.

"The cheerleaders had new outfits last year?" Todd asked.

"You didn't notice?" Brian sounded genuinely puzzled.

Moni paused before biting the doughnut she was holding and raised an eyebrow at me. I'd known her long enough to catch the meaning of that look: *When did Brian start notic-ing cheerleaders?* Not the best development, especially when you considered that somewhere around homecoming, Brian and Moni had gone from "just friends" to something a touch friendlier.

"I guess it doesn't matter how big a boy's brain is," I whispered, "it can still be derailed by an insanely short skirt." But Moni wasn't paying attention.

"Whatever," she said to the group. "There's nothing so special about cheerleading. I mean, even Bethany and I could do that."

"Do . . . what?" Todd and I said at the same time.

"You know. Ready . . . okay!" Moni bounced on the balls of her feet, like she might break into a display of spirit fingers at any moment.

"You mean," I said, going along with it (because annoying Todd was my favorite sport), "you and me trying out for the varsity cheerleading squad?"

"Who says we can't?"

Ummm, *technically*, no one.

Todd knelt at the edge of the stage and frowned down at us, his oversize dork glasses slipping down his nose. "You have got to be kidding."

Yeah. What he said.

But out loud, I agreed with Moni. "Think about it, Todd. We could petition to expand cheerleading to support the debate team. The chess club, even. You know, *Gambit to the left, castle to the right, endgame, endgame, now in sight!*"

Moni giggled. Brian, still lazing near the back of the room, snorted in appreciation. A few of the other guys took up the cheer.

You know how in Greek mythology, Medusa could turn anyone who looked at her into stone? At that moment she had nothing on Todd Emerson. Lucky for me, the bell rang.

Or maybe not so lucky—Todd and I shared first-period honors history.

We all filed from the Little Theater and straight into the heart of the gauntlet, together. Todd had this theory about strength in numbers. It was one of the reasons he collected the nerds, the debate dorks, the third-tier drama geeks, the lowly and lonely freshmen, and invited them all to his house for Geek Night every Saturday. As a combined force, we could breach the gauntlet. Whereas if any one of us tried it alone? Suicide.

And it worked. Mostly. Chantal Simmons stepped back immediately, but then, she probably didn't want smart cooties on her three-hundred-dollar coral-colored peep-toe pumps.

Some of the boys still chanted the chess cheer as we passed a few members of the varsity basketball team. Seniors Ryan Nelson and Luke Vandenberg stood with Jack Paulson. All three of them looked up, like the chant was their cue to rush the court and play. Only Jack seemed to notice we weren't cheering for them. He frowned.

I wanted to turn, go back and tell him that we weren't making fun of him. But it was too late; the crowd had already taken me along in its tide. Maybe I could explain when I saw him in Independent Reading class.

Oh, who was I kidding? I could barely respond when Jack graced me with a few words across the classroom aisle. I'd never be able to explain, not now, not then. Even so, I turned around for one last look. Instead of Jack, I locked eyes with Todd. He handed me a Krispy Kreme—a slightly battered Krispy Kreme, but one from the middle of the box. It was still warm.

"Checkmate," he said.

The bank's time and temperature display flashed: 10:46 P.M./29°. Only in Minnesota could it be this cold just four days past Halloween. All of us—me, Moni, Todd, Brian, plus assorted members of the chess club, debate team, and Math League—shivered outside the Games 'n More video store.

Light spilled from the warm movie theater lobby a few doors down, but I knew the huge sign on its door read NO LOITERING. It was the strip mall and hypothermia for us. And there were still seventy-four frigid minutes before the midnight release of the latest shoot-'em-up video game.

What a way to spend a Saturday night.

We huddled together on a bus-stop bench. Todd lounged on my right—in his Nietzsche "that which does not kill me, makes me stronger" mode—pretending that the cold had no effect on him. Brian sat to Moni's left. Every five minutes he scooted a millimeter closer to her. The rest of the guys took turns standing in line. Apparently some geeks were more equal than others.

But that was no surprise. In these boys' world, status was measured in grade point averages and frag counts. Todd and Brian were at the top of both those lists. And Moni and me? We weren't there because we were dying to buy some dumb video game the first second it dropped.

"The category is famous first lines," Todd said. "You go first, Reynolds."

Of all the books I'd read (1,272 since I started keeping

count) I couldn't think of a single opening line. I was pretty sure that meant my brain was frozen.

"I've got one if she doesn't," a member of the chess club offered.

"It's Reynolds, numbnuts. She's got one," Todd said in my defense. Some of the animosity I'd felt toward him for moving Geek Night from the toasty confines of his basement to the icy tundra that was Prairie Stone Plaza softened.

"Okay, how about," I began, but my brain was still iced up. I'd have to go with my fallback—an oldie, a goodie, my favorite. "'It is a truth universally acknowledged, that a single man in possession of a good fortune must be in want of a . . .'?"

"Too easy," said Moni over the top of her gas-station cappuccino. "C'mon, guys," she said. "You have to know this one."

"Uh . . . it's . . . it's . . . ," Todd struggled. "Give me a second . . . er . . . Brian?"

"Is that your final answer?" Moni snorted, causing the steam from her cup to fog her glasses and loosen a curl so that it fell onto her forehead.

Brian grinned at her, or did until a burst of giggles echoed down the plaza.

The late movie had just let out, and a group of kids hurried to their cars. Clouds of breath billowed ahead of them, partially hiding their faces, but the giggle sounded like Cassidy Anderson, the "Omigod!" was unmistakably Traci Olson's, and the clipped, condescending "Check it" could belong to none other than Chantal Simmons.

"What was the question again?" Brian asked, his attention focused near the theater's exit.

I repeated, "'It is a truth universally acknowledged, that a single man in possession of a good fortune must be in want of a . . .'?"

"A . . . cheerleader?" Brian answered, his face still turned toward the movie crowd.

Now it was Todd's turn to snort. "Yeah, that's it. Final answer."

I thought it was funny, but Moni's face fell. She hopped to her feet and took a step away from the group.

"What'd I say?" asked Brian. His round cheeks, already pink, grew red.

"Cheerleader, good one." Todd leaned across me and smacked Brian on the arm. "Can I quote you on that?" He made a show of pulling out his iPhone to record Brian's words and probably the latitude and longitude at which they were uttered.

"Moni, come back," I said. "Please."

"Yeah," Todd said, a little too loud. "Besides, it's my turn next, and I've got a good one. 'A long time ag—'"

"*Star Wars*? Again?" I wasn't the only one who groaned.

"Okay," Todd said, "how about: 'In the week bef—'"

"*Dune*," I interrupted.

"No way, Reynolds. There is no way you could've known that."

Todd was way more predictable than he liked to believe. So was Moni. She still stood a few feet away, her arms crossed over her chest, a glare aimed at Brian.

"Really, Moni. I'm sorry," Brian said as he started to stand. His voice rose in volume and pitch, drowning out me, and even Todd. "I don't know what I said that was so—"

"Trouble in Nerdland?" A pair of teal, pumpkin, and tan ballet flats appeared only inches from my feet. I didn't have to look up to know who it was. No one in Prairie Stone had a finer shoe wardrobe than Chantal Simmons.

Todd sputtered but gave up before saying anything coherent. Brian froze, half-sitting, half-standing, his posture apelike. Moni tapped a toe but didn't say a word. I kept my eyes on the sidewalk. It was better that way.

Chantal and crew stepped off the curb, and a few freshmen math whizzes stared after them. No one said a word until the girls were inside their car and slipping down the frosty street. Then one of the boys let out a low whistle.

"Cheerleaders," his friend said wistfully.

Moni threw her cappuccino into the trash. The cup rattled, and a couple of boys jumped.

"Really, you guys," she said. "What have they got that we haven't got?"

"I assume that's a rhetorical question," said Todd.

When Brian joined the chorus of heh-heh-hehs, Moni scooped up her mittens and her Sudoku book and clomped down the sidewalk. I hurried after her. Brian tried to follow, but Moni shot him a look that, I swear, dropped the temperature another ten degrees.

"I'm serious," she said when I caught up to her. "What *do* they have that we don't?"

She stopped in front of Waterman's Women's Wear and made a slow turn in the display window's reflection.

I didn't know what to tell her. I was pretty sure we weren't ugly. Moni was bouncy and petite, curvy in the right places. I was taller and a little too thin, but not in a size-zero-starlet sort of way. Moni's bright blond curls were the opposite of my straight, dark bob. I hugged myself against the cold. "Maybe it's the pom-poms," I said.

"Yeah." Moni pushed her arms straight forward, then pulled them quickly back. She thrust them up in the shape of a V, then did a swivel-hipped pivot thing and checked her reflection once again.

Just when I thought she was going to go all Dance Dance Revolution on me, she stopped and stared at our images in the glass.

"Maybe."

The following Monday morning, Moni's brain seemed as fogged over as her glasses. I had to remind her twice before she pulled off her Camp SohCahToa hat and stowed it in her locker. At lunch she walked right past our meet-up spot and would have glided into the gauntlet if I hadn't grabbed her shoulder.

It wasn't until last hour that I really started to worry. Most of the geek squad had been excused from eighth-period classes. We were all in the Little Theater, up on the stage, getting ready to start practice for the National Honor Society induction ceremony. Mr. Wilker, the NHS advisor, had just assigned each of us a sophomore inductee to shepherd through the program when the door to the theater opened.

Cassidy Anderson (senior, cheerleader, gauntlet girl) stepped inside, bringing in a thin stream of light with her.

The radiance followed her as she bounced down the aisle to the foot of the stage.

She handed Mr. Wilker a note. "Thank you, Miss Anderson," he said, then turned his attention back to our group under the lights.

"Um," Cassidy said, "I sort of need that right away."

Mr. Wilker paused and glanced at the note. "My grade book is back in the classroom. I'll have to check that first."

Moni left her sophomore and nudged me. "I bet she needs proof she's not flunking," she said. "Cheerleading tryouts, you know."

No, I did not know. I didn't really care, either. Except that Cassidy still hadn't left. Every second she delayed practice made it more likely I wouldn't have a chance to finish my Life at Prairie Stone column before the newspaper staff meeting after school. I stole a glance at Todd. If I didn't turn in my column, he'd make my life miserable. That is, if he could pull himself out of the hormone-induced rapture that seemed to coincide with Cassidy's arrival.

Dork.

And he wasn't the only one. While Mr. Wilker negotiated with Cassidy, I took a look at the boys onstage. Their combined IQ was probably close to thirty gazillion, but no one would believe it if they saw them in this state. All that chest puffing and gut-sucking-in-ing, and Brian—was he actually slobbering? Really. They might as well have been Neanderthals.

I turned back to Moni, certain that she'd spit out a suitably scathing, sarcastic remark. Instead she blinked, then turned her head from Brian to Cassidy and back again. Beneath us, Mr. Wilker attempted to get the practice under way again.

"Cassidy," he said finally, "I'll meet you in my room after school."

"But—but—," Cassidy whined. She blew a bubble with the gum she was chewing. After it popped, she huffed, "I guess you can just have someone bring it to me."

Fifteen male hands shot into the air as if powered by rockets.

Cassidy turned and headed up the slope toward the exit. When she opened the door, the lobby lights framed her body in silhouette and accented the shine of her hair. She paused as if posing, then whipped around to address us.

"Hey, losers," she said. "Take a picture next time. It might last longer."

With that, the door whooshed closed and plunged us all into darkness.

"That's it," Moni whispered at my side. "We're going to do it."

"Do what?" I whispered back.

"Try out for cheerleading."

"What!" I said, forgetting for a moment how good the acoustics in the Little Theater could be.

"Miss Reynolds?" said Mr. Wilker. "Something you'd like to share with the rest of us?"

I shook my head, but on the inside I was thinking of all sorts of things I'd like to share with Moni, the main one being, *Was she out of her freaking mind?*

Check Your Pulse

Simon & Schuster's **Check Your Pulse** e-newsletter offers current updates on the hottest titles, exciting sweepstakes, and exclusive content from your favorite authors.

Visit **SimonSaysTEEN.com** to sign up, post your thoughts, and find out what every avid reader is talking about!

Margaret K. McElderry Books

Simon & Schuster
Books for Young Readers

SIMON PULSE